THE PALM SPRINGS TALES

BOOK ONE: FAMILY TIES

Geoff Holter

ISBN: 1492278866
ISBN 13: 9781492278863
Library of Congress Control Number: 2013915929
CreateSpace Independent Publishing Platform
North Charleston, South Carolina

PROLOGUE

Incest, multiple brutal murders, sexual mutilation, bondage, Sadomasochism, all in the peaceful and idyllic setting of America's desert paradise and all wrapped in a decidedly gay sensibility.

Beverly Pickle was living an idyllic retirement with his partner of forty seven years. Life was peaceful and happy and almost perfect. Until it wasn't.

At once a murder mystery and a very black comedy, Family Ties shows a side of Palm Springs seldom experienced by visitors.

From their perch in the palm grove high above the pool the crows watched the dance of darkness and light in the water below. Something sparkled at the edge of a shadow. A breeze rustled the palms and the moon moved towards its setting in the west as the first streaks of light dusted the eastern sky.

The shadow moved with the current but never quite surfaced as it passed in front of lights and took form as arms, legs, torso and a great black halo of hair. A ruby red ribbon trailed behind.

In the distance a dog barked and further away still, a siren screamed. The palms swayed in the breeze as the crows cawed and watched.

****

I awoke to more than the usual noise of leaf blowers. Voices were coming from the pool area. The still hot air in the bedroom was disrupted only slightly by the ceiling fan and promised another scorcher of a day. Shards of light pierced cracks in the shutters and shot beams of dust particles through the half light. One landed an accusative finger on a framed photo of John and me. I forced myself up and shook my head to clear the haze from last night's wine.

Peeking out a shuttered window I saw police officers leaning over the pool, seemingly trying to fish something out. Although she was out of view, I heard the distinctive voice of Cora the building manager. John, my partner of forty seven years, was still dead to the world, emitting little snoring noises and grunts as he breathed.

****

The call came in at 6:13 a.m. It was relayed from the emergency call centre and reported a possible homicide at Caballeros Estates on Avenida Caballeros. By the time it reached Mike Kruger's desk he had finished his first coffee and was just starting to peruse the arrest records from the previous night. He grabbed his jacket and headed for the car. Caballeros Estates was only a few blocks over and he arrived in minutes. Two other squad cars pulled up behind him. Waiting for them at the front gate was a tiny, white haired woman and a portly bearded man. Both were enveloped in a haze of smoke as they puffed steadily on cigarettes. She introduced herself as the property manager and he as the chairman of the Home Owners' Association. While taking his dog for an early morning walk he discovered a body floating in one of the swimming pools.

They made their way through the gardens to a pool surrounded by a grove of very tall palms. From high up in the trees crows cawed. The pool lights shone through the early morning darkness and illuminated an undulating shadow beneath the surface. Mike waved everyone back as he approached the edge. The shadow was a body and it was trailing a long sash of blood in the water.

****

By the time I pulled on my kimono and sandals and made it out to the pool there was already a small gathering of neighbours, some sipping coffee in silence while others spoke to each other in urgent whispers. A plastic tarp covered something at the north end of the pool. A single, shoeless foot protruded from one end and a hand with a distinctive ring hung out the side. The water was the colour of fuchsia. At the far end a black shoe bobbed in a whirlpool of dead leaves and bougainvillea.

One of the policemen called out from behind the Jacuzzi. We moved in that direction but were waved back. The policeman put on gloves and lifted a hatchet very carefully from behind a lemon tree. He placed it in a plastic bag and continued to search the area.

****

Mike looked across the pool at the growing crowd of residents. They were a typical bunch for this type of complex in Palm Springs, composed mostly of older women and gay men. Several had dogs with them. Most looked horrified although some were acting as if they were on a movie set. One old guy in a worn robe was chatting endlessly to anyone who would listen. His eyes affected a startled theatricality as he moved through the crowd with his balding head tilted back in a gesture of perpetual surprise.

Somewhere in the background opera was playing. It wafted through the trees before settling over the pool. It came from a patio that was protected from public view by dense foliage and a locked heavy metal gate.

2

It was one of those days when the desert sun turns asphalt to soft tar and the highway oozes toxins that rise visibly into the almost viscous air. The road from Vegas was never pretty but on this blistering day it was at its most desolate. Sixteen wheelers screamed by Lucy's ancient Volkswagen camper, each time creating a hot draft that nearly blew her off the road. She clung to the wheel, every muscle in her body tense and completely focussed on getting to Palm Springs.

Life had not been kind to Lucy. Married to an alcoholic trucker for thirteen years and living in trailer parks in the seedier parts of Vegas, what, at age 16, seemed like a good escape from the tyranny of her ultra religious family in Idaho, turned quickly into an American nightmare of domestic rape and beatings. He wouldn't leave her alone even when she was pregnant. The first baby, a boy, died within hours of birth. The second, a girl, survived and now at twelve, looked just like her thuggish father. The third, a boy, was already showing signs of a troubled life ahead. For Lucy they weren't family at all, just a kind of millstone that kept grinding her down.

One night after her shift at the IHOP Lucy turned into a roadhouse that was halfway between work and the trailer. She settled at the bar and asked for a Bud while listening to Tammy Wynette on the jukebox. Her reflection stared back from the smoky mirror behind the bar. She was twenty nine years old but looked forty. Her Farah Fawcett hairdo hung limply after a day of waitressing in a barely air conditioned café, its ash blonde colour obviously from a bottle. A thin line of mascara ran down by her left eye, somehow making the false eyelashes look enormous. Her lipstick was slightly askew, something she tried to rectify with a cocktail napkin. Crows feet punctuated both eyes.

Thirteen years of marriage, three pregnancies, two children she barely knew and a husband she detested and feared: this was the sum total of Lucy's share of the American dream. She was exhausted and depressed.

A heavy set woman sat down beside her, pulled the ashtray over and lit a cigarette. She introduced herself as Marsha and offered to buy Lucy a second beer. Anything to prolong time away from the trailer was welcome and Lucy accepted gladly. Two hours later she was in the back of the cab of Marsha's truck with her blouse open, her skirt around her waist and Marsha's head between her legs. She had never experienced an orgasm before. It would not be her last.

After her brief encounter with Marsha Lucy became quite adept at picking up tricks at truck stops. She cultivated her role as the femme while learning how to pleasure her butch companions. It was one such encounter that brought her to Abby who, unlike most of her other tricks, was simply stopping on the outskirts of Vegas as she made her way home to Palm Springs. Something clicked and for the next eight months they met regularly in a string of cheap motel rooms that Abby rented by the hour.

Back at the trailer things were going from bad to worse. While her husband was usually too drunk to notice her absences, he did comment on the strange smells on her body. At some level he knew something had changed and that made him even more violent. Lucy knew how this would end. One night he would go too far and kill her. It was as simple as that. When Abby first raised the possibility of Lucy coming to live with her in Palm Springs it seemed crazy. But, as the weeks passed and the violence at the trailer increased, it became not only plausible but essential.

Lucy plotted her escape carefully. There was a secret bank account where she had stashed a few hundred dollars. She had no suitcase but a large, plastic bag was really all she needed for what she would take. The old Volkswagen camper was bought with money she earned and she used it every day to drive to work. One day she just kept going.

Abby's Cathedral City trailer was the first of several homes Lucy inhabited in the Palm Springs area. There was also a string of low end jobs waiting tables or cleaning third rate motel rooms. One night after downing several beers she backed her Volkswagen into a Mercedes convertible that was parked next to her outside the girl bar in Cathedral City. Its owner, Pearl was a retired realtor and took an instant shine to this beat up young woman. Two weeks later Lucy packed her few belongings and moved in with Pearl in her south Palm Springs bungalow. She lived there for the next thirty eight years. When Pearl died of cancer she left her estate to Adele as Lucy now called herself. It included several run down condos in Caballeros Estates that Pearl rented for as much as possible while spending absolutely nothing on their upkeep. Her tenants were mostly drug addicts, prostitutes, dealers, pimps and anyone else with quick cash and a need for anonymity.

Adele didn't like living in the house without Pearl and two months after her death she sold it and moved into one of her Caballeros Estates condos.

3

The closing chords of Nessun Dorma settled gently over Jeffery's reclining body.

No, no, sulla tua bocca lo dirò
quando la luce splenderà!
Ed il mio bacio scioglierà il silenzio
che ti fa mia!
(Il nome suo nessun saprà!...
e noi dovrem, ahime, morir!)
Dilegua, o notte!
Tramontate, stelle!
Tramontate, stelle!
All'alba vincerò!
vincerò, vincerò!

.

He held the silk robe tightly against his throat and imagined himself the heartless Chinese princess. His reflection stared back from the cracked Chinoiserie mirror leaning on the adjacent table. His face had the texture of old tanned leather but he could still detect the pretty boy behind that mask. Most of his blond hair remained although sunlight exposed streaks of silver that blended into a moustache that was completely white and softened the rest of his face. His slim muscular body attested to years of working out. Best of all were the eyes. Those green, bewitching cat eyes that entrapped so many gullible tourists in Vegas. A smile briefly flitted across his face at the memory.

Through his eyelashes the early morning sun sparkled in tiny flashes like exploding flashbulbs. Without fully opening his eyes he found the remnants of his martini, pulled it to his lips and sucked in the warm gin nectar. He settled comfortably into the faded chintz fabric of the ancient chaise lounge. Somewhere in the background there were voices, but far away as the opening strains of Casta Diva floated from the CD player.

Casta Diva, che inargenti
queste sacre antiche piante,
a noi volgi il bel sembiante
senza nube e senza vel...

His mind drifted to his days in Vegas with Christian when they were the toast of the town or at least that part that was attracted to slim, tanned, androgynous show boys. Things were, well, if not simpler then, at least more glamorous. Six nights a week on stage in skin tight outfits competing with showgirls. The after show cocktails; the invitations to late night assignations and the sense that, any minute, a dark, handsome stranger would walk in, sweep him off his feet and carry him away to a life of glamour and sophistication, probably on the French Riviera.

Jeffery's gin soaked brain couldn't quite recall when the glamour of Vegas began to fade and he realized there was no dark handsome stranger and the nights of grease paint, tight fitting costumes and quickie blow jobs in the back seats of cars was as good as it was going to get. Was it him or Christian who came up with the idea of moving to Palm Springs and opening a men's only, clothing optional gay resort? Leaving was as easy as quitting his job, packing a couple of suitcases and driving west. Except for Christian, there was no one in Vegas he cared for. He hadn't seen his sister or father in years and his mother disappeared mysteriously when he was a boy.

They had enough money to buy a rundown motel close to downtown Palm Springs. They named it Innsext and, in time, turned it into a success, catering to middle aged men from Middle America who's every day lives involved families, white picket fences and bible study and who came to Palm Springs to get laid by as many men as possible as quickly as possible. There was a fine line between running a hotel and running a bath house and they tread it carefully. That could have gone on indefinitely if it weren't for Christian's drug habit. In time, Innsext became known as the place to buy drugs and get laid, sometimes as part of the same transaction. This didn't go unnoticed by the police. When the final raid occurred Christian was so stoned he accidentally spilled his entire stash of meth and ecstasy into the lap of a police officer. He was now serving eight years in a federal penitentiary somewhere in Alabama. After a brief investigation, Jeffery was cleared of all charges. He sold the resort and rented a small condo in Caballeros Estates.

4

Cora was having a sleepless night. Aside from her chronic emphysema, she couldn't stop thinking about the argument with that bitch Adele. The old dyke actually threatened her, saying she would buy her mortgage from the bank and evict her. Times were tough and she was behind in her payments but the thought that she could actually lose her home of twenty years had never occurred to her. And to make matters worse, lose it to her old nemesis. Shortly after one she got up, lit a cigarette and went out to her terrace. The first cooing of the doves made the warm night seem comforting and safe. Then, over towards the north end of the complex she heard voices, voices that got louder in what seemed like an argument. She couldn't make out whether they were male or female before they went silent. It was probably some of the boys coming home from the bars. She snuffed out her cigarette and went back to bed.

Cora's life had been hard. It started out well with loving and supportive parents and seemed on a happy trajectory when she married her high school sweetheart and, in short order, had three kids, two boys and a girl. Everything came off the road when a sudden heart attack killed her husband when her youngest was not yet one. After that, Cora was super mom and bread winner. She didn't always hit home runs on either score and now, at 75, remained in contact with only one child, her gay son. While she loved him dearly, she had long ago given up hoping for a successful life for him. Whether because of drugs, bad boyfriends or run ins with the law, he was always a cause for worry. She bought her small apartment at Caballeros Estates although it required a large mortgage and when the opportunity to become manager presented she took it, knowing the extra money would come in handy. So, here she was, moving inexorably into old age, working harder than most people half her age and, most of all, alone.

****

Neal was dreaming about Rex. His long time, faithful companion was dead, buried secretly in the garden created as a memorial to a deceased member of the HOA board. Rex, who barked occasionally but otherwise wouldn't hurt a fly, was found frothing at the mouth and semi conscious by the south pool two weeks ago. He'd been poisoned and Neal was certain he knew by whom. Adele hated Rex and was always complaining about him being off his leash. The last time they'd spoken she practically threatened to do away with him. And now he was dead leaving Neal and Sadie to mourn.

Neal woke from the dream with tears streaming down his face. It was 5:20 and the Mocking Bird was just beginning its early morning mating song. Sadie saw he was awake and started whining. It was a bit early for her walk but sleep was over so he pulled on a T-shirt and shorts, grabbed her leash and headed for the door.

It was very still and dark outside. Although the searing heat of the day had subsided, the temperature still hovered around 80. With no one around he didn't bother to leash Sadie and she galloped off in the direction of the north pool. As he approached he saw her down on her haunches looking into the water. Then he saw why. A body was circulating with the current. Neal was too startled to investigate further. He grabbed Sadie, leashed her and headed for Cora's door.

****

The banging wouldn't stop. In the dream her son was trying to tell her something but she couldn't make out what through the noise. The dream and the noise began to diverge, one fading the other becoming louder and more intrusive. She opened her eyes with a start and heard someone calling her name. The knocking became more insistent. When she opened the door there stood Neal, restraining Sadie and looking very agitated.

It took a couple of minutes for Neal to get the message out. First there was something about a body and then one of the pools and then blood. Finally it registered, there was a body floating in the north pool. Cora lit a cigarette, grabbed her cell phone and headed for the pool. Sure enough, there was a body floating face down, trailed by a lot of blood. As she moved closer Cora recognized the figure. Adele. A strange guilty tingle went up her spine and, just for a moment, she nearly laughed. She closed her eyes, focussed and dialled 911.

5

Susan had just ordered her second bourbon when she noticed the young man looking at her. It was a look she hadn't received in years. Now, on her fiftieth birthday a young man, well relatively young anyway, was giving her that look. One minute she was mourning the passing of her life and the next she was the object of someone's lust.

He came over and smiled awkwardly. She also attempted a smile back. When he asked to join her she flushed but gave a kind of nod. His name was Mathew, or Mat, and he was drinking bourbon too. Although fifteen years her junior he seemed to find her attractive. They woke up hung-over and in her bed the next morning.

Mat didn't have much of a career. For a time he sold life insurance, then real estate and, finally, cars. Somehow they managed to scrape together the money to buy a small condo in Palm Springs where, every weekend, they would escape from their West Covina apartment. Twenty years and much bourbon later they still made the trek down I-10 to Palm Springs every Friday night.

Their Palm Springs condo was in Caballeros Estates where Adele befriended them. One night in 2007 the three of them were drinking on their patio when Adele reached over and placed her hand on Susan's bare leg. Everyone was pretty drunk and, for a few moments, nobody seemed to notice. Then Adele slid her hand up Susan's leg towards her thigh all the while continuing the conversation with Mat who became silent. When Susan pulled her leg away, Adele's hand followed. Finally Mat said: "what the fuck are you doing?". Suddenly

Adele was no longer the inebriated friendly neighbour and said something about Susan needing a good fuck with a woman. Before the words were fully out Mat was on his feet, grabbing her by the hair and throwing her against the wall. Adele came back like an enraged hyena and it was only Mat's considerable bulk that prevented him from being bowled over. He finally shoved her out the gate, shouting something about a "lesbian cunt". Adele called the police and charged Mat with assault. After some negotiation the charges were dropped.

6

Luis snuggled deeper under the covers, pulling Chita closer and enveloping her warm, scented body with his arms and legs. He ran his hand down her back to the swelling where her buttocks began all the while tonguing her nipples and belly down to the warm, moist area of her panocha. He spread her legs and rubbed his face against the rough black hair. He moved up to mount her while holding her so tightly she seemed to merge with his body. His hard-on was almost painful. Then she was gone. For a moment he was suspended high up in the air above the bed and then he fell at a terrifying speed. He forced himself awake and sat bolt upright. Next to him the bed was empty. Then he remembered. They had taken her away. Three uniformed immigration police and now she was detained somewhere outside of San Diego waiting to be deported to Mexico.

Pedro, their little black mutt with only three legs and a stub of a tail jumped on the bed and whined. He missed her as much as Luis. Luis scratched him behind the ears and Pedro responded with a half hearted wag of what was left of his tail. As he did so his three legs had difficulty keeping him upright and he tumbled over onto the place where Chita should have been sleeping.

Luis had worked so hard since coming to America, first as an illegal and then, after five years, with a green card. He laboured from 7 in the morning until 6 every night clearing and pruning and cleaning the grounds at Caballeros Estates. He was so lonely and when Chita entered his life it was like a gift from God. And now that gift was cruelly snatched away.

He still wasn't sure how it happened except that that woman had something to do with it. He remembered her looking at Chita in an odd way, a way that just wasn't right. And then, when Chita came upon her naked in the Jacuzzi, the woman propositioned her. Chita, simple peasant girl that she was, had no idea what was happening and mentioned it to Cora. After that, things were a bit of blur. Within days uniformed officers came to his door and took her away. And now he was alone again.

7

Why would they want to interview me? And first? I didn't see anything. I was fast asleep with John and then woke to noise out by the pool. Nothing else. And why do I have to go to the police station for the interview? Aren't they supposed to do this at the scene of the crime? Cora said not to worry, that everyone was going to be interviewed, but why me first?

I can't decide what to wear. I don't want to look too gay but, on the other hand, looking too sombre might arouse suspicion that I was trying to hide something. And why aren't they interviewing John? Not that I'd want him to go through this at his age but I don't know any more than he does. And I have heart problems. They've already had to replace one of my stents and another could go at any time. I mean, I could keel over dead in the middle of the interview.

Fitted jeans might be appropriate and a pink polo shirt. A scarf maybe? I wonder if I should wear any jewellery? Maybe a bracelet.

I mean there are lots of people with reasons to kill Adele. But I'm not one of them. Yes, she owns both condos above us, or at least used to, and, yes, when I asked her to have her tenant stop sliding his furniture across the deck above my bedroom she wasn't very helpful. And there was the incident with the tenant who jammed her dog's poop down the drain, plugging it and leading to an unsightly brown stain on our ceiling. That certainly wasn't very nice but not something one would kill over. And of course there was that time she claimed our parking stall, even painted her number over ours but that got worked out too. Anyway I couldn't hurt a flea. Speaking of which, there was also the infestation of bed bugs her last tenant left us.

God, this is awful. I'm a wreck. And already sweating. They'll think I'm hiding something.

****

Mike doubted the kid would ever be a good cop but he sure was a keener. The fact he had good computer skills was a bonus but the thought of him packing iron was certainly unsettling. He was from Bakersfield, a recent graduate of the police academy and ready to make his mark. He was also the sole assistant assigned to work with Mike on the Caballeros homicide. Times were tough and even police departments were downsizing.

They had prepared a list of residents they wanted to interview and the first one was due at the station at nine that morning. Mike decided to let the kid conduct the interview while he watched from the other side of the two way mirror. That way he could assess both the kid and the interviewee.

****

Bakersfield is a little bit of the Bible belt dropped in the middle of California. With God, guns and Republican as its mantra it looks with disgust at Babylon by the Bay to the north and the fleshpot of Los Angeles to the south. In every way it defies the popular image of California and its streets are dotted with churches and other houses of worship of every possible persuasion.

This is the world that Zachariah Mathew Joseph Smith was born into on March 28, 1989. He was a third generation citizen of Bakersfield, his grandparents having arrived as Mormon missionaries in the worst days of the depression and dust bowl. His father ran a small electronics repair shop and his mother did the book keeping as well as raising Zach, as he became known and his three older brothers. Their life revolved around the shop, the Church of Jesus Christ of Latter Day Saints and the Republican Party.

Zach was a sickly child with none of the athleticism of his three siblings. While they were playing sports he spent hours alone in his bedroom on the computer. He was a geek before it was fashionable.

Zach absorbed the politics of his parents and church and when "Gay Marriage" was first legalized in California he shared their disgust. When Proposition 8 was proposed he was in the vanguard of the campaign to get it on the ballot and then to pass it, spending hours on street corners and at shopping malls passing out leaflets and telling anyone who would listen that "Gay Marriage" was an abomination before God. When Proposition 8 passed he felt pride in the role he had played, seeing the outcome as a vindication of God's will.

Zach always wanted to be a policeman. When, after finishing high school, he had a chance to attend the police academy, he jumped at it. While hardly a robust performer in the training, his computer skills served him well and he graduated. The next problem was finding a posting and, given the virtual collapse of the state economy, that proved harder than expected. Finally, after months of filing applications, he got a nibble from Palm Springs.

Zach didn't know much about Palm Springs except what he had seen in movies or read about in super market tabloids. As far as he could tell, it was populated by movie stars, was in a desert and was relatively close to Los Angeles. He arrived for his interview in the middle of August. The town was completely deserted as the blast furnace heat seared anything exposed to it.

He got the job and started his career as a member of the Palm Springs Police Department on September 1, 2011. The first time he put on his uniform Zach strode to the nearest mirror expecting to see a confident, robust man in uniform. Instead, he saw what looked like a runty kid in an adult's uniform. The hat made his head look tiny and his grey eyes created a really creepy effect staring out from under the brim. The revolver and radio strapped to his sides almost doubled the width of his hips. There was little reason to think his skinny arms could handle either. He was deflated but determined. He thrust out his flat chest, tilted his head back and visualized the tough, wiry cop he planned to become.

Palm Springs was very different from Bakersfield. For one thing it was filled with really old people and homosexuals (he was trying to shed the term "fags"). Except for a couple of months in the spring, it was mostly dead and the only police work involved a drunk pissing on someone's bougainvillea or a granny tripping over a planter. Once in a while, after a heavy rain a tourist might get swept away in a flash flood after ignoring the warning signs. But all that resulted in was recovery, not solving anything. That all changed when he was assigned to assist inspector Kruger on the Caballeros murder case.

****

I approached the police station with great trepidation. Even though it was only a short walk from the condo and I stopped at Pinocchio's for brunch, I was soaked with perspiration, particularly under my arms where the soft pink polo shirt showed great arcs of darkness stretching down both sides. I opened the door, gritted my teeth, thrust my shoulders back and walked into the cool interior. My nostrils were immediately assaulted by the acrid smell of Pine Sol. An officious little Hispanic woman eyed me suspiciously from behind the counter. It seemed that her primary duty was to repel anyone who was going to take any of her time. I positioned myself at the counter right in front of her. She glared up in silence, challenging me to justify this intrusion on her time and turf.

I cleared my throat and spoke in an irritatingly high, nasally voice.

"My name is Beverly Pickle. I have an appointment with police officer Kruger."

"How do you spell 'Beverly'"?

"BEVERLY"

"Oh, the way a woman would." She barely suppressed a snigger.

She turned to her computer screen, entered a few keys and waited. Then she turned to me and spoke in an alarmingly loud voice.

"You're connected to the Caballeros Estates murder?"

I was aghast. I was no such thing. I was just here to help. I had been summoned for an interview.

"I wouldn't say connected but I am here to be interviewed."

She snorted contemptuously and waived in the general direction of some chairs. I went and sat down. There was only one other person in the waiting area: an extremely scruffy and unclean looking old man who let off a very unpleasant, unwashed odour even from a distance. He stared directly at me. I gave a slight, and I hoped dismissive, nod. That's when he broke into a toothless grin and moved to the chair next to me.

He put out his hand.

"My name is Fred, what's yours?"

I couldn't avoid the handshake and then was afraid to touch any other part of my body with the now contaminated hand. I tried to avoid the question but he stared so intently at me I finally blurted out "Beverly".

"Huh. What did you say?"

"I said "Beverly"."

He gave me a quizzical look and asked "You are a guy aren't you?"

"I most certainly am." That seemed to satisfy him and he moved even closer.

"So, you're involved in the murder of the old gal over on Caballeros are you?"

"I'm not "involved" as you describe it at all. I live there part of the time and they just want to talk to me about some general background".

The old guy cackled emitting the smell of garlic, onion, stale booze and god knows what else. I needed a shower. I thought I might just expire on the spot. I noticed a blond haired older man talking to the receptionist and looking my way. He came towards me, his hand extended.

"Mr Pickle. I'm Officer Kruger. Thanks for coming in. Please come this way."

I was so relieved to be removed from the presence of my scruffy interrogator I forgot momentarily that the real interrogation was in front of me. I followed the officer down a short hallway and into a windowless room with a table and two chairs. One wall was a mirror.

****

The kid was ecstatic when he learned he was handling the interview. He'd been trained of course and had watched many such interviews on TV over the years but this was the first time that he, Zachariah Smith, would play the leading role. He watched as Officer Kruger offered a seat to the guy and then left the room to join him next door.

"The guy's pretty nervous Zach."

Zach looked through the glass at the old queer. He was fidgeting with a bracelet and stretching his neck as if trying to relieve tension. His eyes had a wide, startled quality. In fact, he looked quite alarmed.

"Do you think he's a homosexual sir?"

"I think that's a fair certainty but you need to be very careful not to bring that up. Remember what happened to the guys involved with the raid on Warm Sands last year."

Indeed Zach did remember. In fact, it was pure luck he had not been ensnared in the fall out. The police conducted a stake out in the Warm Sands neighbourhood which was full of homosexual resorts and where there were complaints of men exposing themselves and having sex in public. Zach was disgusted at the behaviour and volunteered for the operation but was rejected when his superiors decided he was not attractive enough to be a decoy. Instead they sent Jimmy Jones who was the kind of guy who always got the cheerleader in school. Jimmy was now on indefinite leave and it was rumoured he was going to be dismissed from the force. The story was that he stood in the middle of the neighbourhood pretending to masturbate for nearly seven hours one night.

Zach sipped his coffee, took a deep breath and opened the door. The old guy's head jerked in a kind of bird like way as he viewed this pimply kid in a uniform.

"Hello. I'm Officer Smith and I'm here to interview you." "You are..." he scanned a sheet attached to his clipboard, pretending not to know Beverly's name..."Mr. Pickle I believe?"

He sat in the chair opposite Beverly, placed an empty notepad on the table and wrote "Beverly Pickle" at the top.

"Now Mr Pickle I have a few questions to ask about the murder over at Caballeros Estates"

"No kidding" I thought. "As if I'm here to discuss Oprah."

"How well did you know the victim?"

"Barely. Hardly at all. I knew who she was but I almost never had contact with her."

"Mm. But it says here she owned the condos above you and you've had some disagreements with her"

I tried to see what he was reading, but failed. An attack of vertigo threatened.

"Well, yes she does own those apartments. In fact she lived in one of them. And, yes there have been a few minor issues over the years but nothing that would lead me to kill her". I was horrified. I couldn't believe I'd blurted out those words.

"No one is suggesting you killed her Mr Pickle. I'm just trying to fill in all the relationships."

I was about to bring up the Eggs Benedict I'd had at Pinocchio's.

"Where were you the night she was killed?"

"At home. In bed. With my husband."

"Your what?"

"My husband"

"I don't understand. In California you can't have a husband. You're a man or at least..." he trailed off before finishing the sentence.

I sensed an opening. "At least what?"

"Nothing. It's just that Proposition 8 passed and there is no such thing as gay marriage in California."

"Well there is in Canada and that is where we are from"

Zach nearly said they should go back there then but stopped just in time.

"Ok. So you say you were with your husband"

"Actually I said I was in bed with my husband" I felt mischievous, the vertigo having subsided. I noticed the young punk reddened slightly.

"Right. And when were you aware of the crime?"

"I have difficulty sleeping you know. I often wake early."

Zach looked at this preening old queen suddenly on his little stage. His head still making bird like movements and his eyes constantly widening in what looked like perpetual surprise. He gestured with his hands which seemed barely connected to his wrists.

"And then I heard a commotion outside. I got up…carefully so as not to disturb John."

"Who's John?"

"My husband. Who else do you think I'd be sleeping with?" There was a note of indignation.

"Dunno. Carry on please."

"Well, as I was saying, I heard a commotion and got out of bed to see what was going on. It's usually very quiet at that time of morning although of late, you know, we've attracted some lower class long term tenants who aren't exactly considerate of the rest of us. Anyway, I peeked out the window and much to my surprise I saw police officers. Although I couldn't see them, I did hear both Neal and Cora's voices. Neal's dog was barking at something in the pool. While I didn't want to seem too nosy, I thought I might be able to help so I put on my robe, got some coffee and went out there. That's when I saw the body."

"Did you know who it was?"

"Not right away. But after a few minutes I noticed the hand and that tasteless gold and turquoise ring that Adele wore all the time."

"Do you know anyone who would've wanted to harm the victim?"

"Well, there's lots of people who didn't like her. I mean she's been throwing her weight around the complex for years. And she can be very mean if she doesn't like you. Also, she doesn't keep her units up, brings all kinds of riff raff in as tenants and opposes any expenditure to improve the place. But, honestly, I can't think of anyone who would kill her. Although…"

"Although what?"

"Well it's probably nothing but she did get rid of that Mexican girl recently and I know Luis is very upset about that. But of course he wouldn't have killed her. I mean, people just don't act that way. At least our people don't. I, I wouldn't expect Mexicans to be any different… would I?"

I looked around nervously, wondering if any Mexicans might be within hearing distance. That's when I remembered the mirrored wall and the many TV shows where people were listened to and observed during interrogations. I flushed.

Zach stood.

"I think that will do for now Mr Pickle. Please stay within the county as we may wish to speak with you further." He gestured to the door.

"Does that mean I can't leave the country now?"

"We'd prefer you didn't until we get a bit more information."

"But I was returning to Vancouver next Monday. Are you saying I can't."

"I'm saying we would like you to remain here for a bit. Thanks for your cooperation." He ushered me out the door.

8

The morning was cool enough for Mike to shut off the engine and open the car windows. The peaks of the San Jacinto Mountains drew a jagged edge against the cerulean sky as the morning sun crept down them towards Palm Springs.

Other than desert dogs racing across the road to disappear into the sagebrush and the steady hum of life over the empty lots, there was no activity on the street. This was a particularly bleak stretch of Arenas where condo developments mixed with empty lots on both sides of the road. The sidewalk stopped and started, depending upon where the developments were and the empty lots were filled with sage and tumble weed that formed barriers along the road.

The funeral was scheduled for 11:00 a.m. at the little Catholic mission church on the corner. Our Lady of Guadeloupe was a squat, one story structure with a tiny chapel. A stone marker at its entrance asked for prayers for unborn babies destroyed in abortions. It's congregation was mostly Hispanic and there was no record of Adele ever attending services there but that is where the funeral was being held.

The hearse was parked alongside the chapel and Mike presumed the casket was already inside. There was still an hour to go and, thus far, no one had turned up. The only activity was two Mexican gardeners planting snap dragons in the little beds in front of the church. Then he noticed someone else. A bag lady was sitting on a railing next to the hearse; her possessions piled high in a grocery cart next to her. That seemed a little odd for the location so Mike decided to investigate.

Her skin was the colour of tanned leather. Two braids of knotted grey hair framed her heavy set face which still showed hints of a long departed prettiness. She wore a loose and torn white t-shirt that hadn't been cleaned in a very long time and her multiple skirts touched the ground. On one foot was a torn and dirty old sneaker while the other was wrapped in a white plastic bag tied tightly around her ankle. She sucked on the stub of a cigarette as she watched his approach with watery and jaundiced eyes.

As he got closer Mike saw she was even dirtier than he had initially thought. There were streaks of dirt and sweat on her face and food stains down her shirt and skirt. She broke into a broad smile revealing two missing upper front teeth.

"Well officer. To what do I owe this honour?"

Her voice was thick with phlegm and she cleared her throat and spat before continuing.

"You want a little nookie maybe, check out my pussy or get a blow job?"

She stood, grabbed her crotch and made pumping motions. The attempt at coquetry collapsed into a garish nightmare.

Mike was repulsed.

"I just want to know what you're doing here?"

"What am I doing here? What are you doing here? This is my home. My little desert oasis. Me and the aborted babies." She cackled and a blast of rancid air washed over him. For a second Mike thought he might retch.

"Do you live here all the time?"

"All the time? Now let me see. Certainly during the season." She let out another cackle at her little joke.

"Where do you sleep?"

"Oh...you do want see my pussy? Over there behind the bush. Want to check it out?"

She gestured to the empty lot across from the church.

"What do you do when you're not here?"

"Well, let's see. I help the neighbours. I get rid of their junk. You know it's disgraceful what people throw out. I find all sorts of treasures in the garbage around here." She gestured towards her cart. "Why only the other day I found a working computer, along with a couple dozen discs, in the dumpster down the road at Caballeros Estates. Terrible the way rich people are ruining the planet with their waste, don't you think?". She gave another toothless grin.

Mike nodded and returned to his car. He made a note about the seemingly harmless bag lady and then turned his attention back to the church. In his side view mirror he saw a small group of people making their way up Arenas from Caballeros. Through the rising heat they seemed a mirage flowing along the sidewalk towards him. In front was a tiny figure dressed entirely in black. As they came nearer Mike recognized her as the manager of Caballeros Estates. Next to her was the portly older man who discovered the body. Behind them were two men. One was the old gay guy they had already interviewed and beside him was a very dignified older man. There were also several people Mike did not recognize. They made their way up the street to the entrance to the church and went inside.

Just as the service was about to begin a large black pickup truck coasted slowly past the church. Mike couldn't see who was inside as the windows were tinted. It nearly stopped and then at the last minute sped up and pulled away to make a turn onto El Segundo. It had Nevada plates.

9

Something woke me. I'd been having a terrible dream about Adele's murder. In it she was sitting on the terrace outside my bedroom gesturing for me to come and join her. Blood was streaming down her face and she was leering at me in a revolting way.

John lay asleep beside me snoring contentedly. Then I heard the noise. I slipped out of bed, pulled on my kimono, and went to the doorway. The terrace furniture and umbrella cast an eerie silhouette but nothing seemed out of place. I heard it again: a muttering sound coming from beyond the wall. I let myself out into the warm night air. A coyote howled somewhere in the distance.

The sound was coming from the other side of the door to the street. It stopped and was replaced by whispers. My throat constricted as I tried to shout "whose there?" Instead, a reedy screech came out. There was silence. My heart was pounding so hard I feared one of the stents would burst. Then the door knob began to turn. My first urge was to flee and alert Cora but then I remembered John dozing peacefully only feet away. I looked desperately for a weapon. The only thing available was the plastic palm tree that seemed such a good idea when I saw it at Revivals. I grabbed it and moved towards the door. The knob was no longer moving. I prayed the lock would hold.

I called John to turn on the light. This time my voice held. Then I heard what sounded like footsteps fading away, car doors slamming and the sudden roar of an engine. The noise receded as the vehicle pulled away into the silent desert night.

****

Who, the hell was pounding on her door at this time of night? Cora grabbed the alarm clock to confirm it was barely 3 a.m. Given the events of the past two weeks she was completely awake as she put on her robe and headed to the front door. Over the banging she could hear Beverly shouting her name hysterically. She opened the door and he nearly fell in. He was dressed in his old kimono and babbling something about intruders, Charles Manson and god knows what else. His eyes were dilated, there was spittle running out the side of his mouth and he was white as a sheet. The more he went on the less sense he made, completely ignoring her requests that he calm down. Finally she reached up and slapped him hard on the face. He stopped dead.

What in god's name is going on? I thwart a break in, go to tell Cora and she slaps me.

"I'm sorry Beverly, but you were out of control. Now sit down and start from the beginning." Cora noticed John trodding up the stairs wearing a sweat suit. He looked confused.

"You slapped me!". I couldn't quite believe it. Again: "You slapped me!".

"I said I'm sorry. Now get on with your goddamned story. It's after 3 a.m. Actually, wait a second while I get a cigarette." She headed for her kitchen.

For a moment I was tempted to rise and stride haughtily out of the room. I mean, really, who was she to talk to me this way. Me, an owner and she our employee. Then I remembered the attempted break in and a chill ran down my spine. Better swallow my pride and get on with it. She returned, smoke in hand.

"OK. Now what happened?"

"Someone tried to break into our patio. I heard them. There was a kind of murmuring . They tried the door. I scared them off."

"How did you scare them off?"

"I shouted at them and turned the lights on." I considered mentioning my weapon but a plastic palm tree didn't quite fit the image I was conjuring.

"Well, then, lets go have a look". Cora produced a flashlight and headed for the door.

Was she mad? For all I knew, serial killers were lurking around the compound, waiting to pounce on their next victim. I tried to object but my voice was dry again. Cora was already halfway out the door and John was following her obediently. I had no choice but to tag along.

We were going past the south pool when I heard something. Cora obviously did too. She stopped, put her finger to her lips and doused the flashlight. The sound came again. It was a sharp crack followed by what sounded like moaning. Silence followed. And then it happed again. It was coming from the direction of Susan and Mat's condo. We edged closer to their patio gate. There was another sharp crack, followed by a moan and then a whimpering sound. Through the locked gate we saw a shadowy figure moving around the living room, but little else. The room was bathed in red light. Cora pulled out her phone and called 911.

****

One of the downsides of being the most junior guy on the force was that you drew most of the graveyard shifts. Zach was killing time looking at the photos from the Caballeros Estates murder when the phone rang. At that time of night there was no one to intercept calls. He picked up and recognized the throaty voice of the little woman who managed Caballeros Estates. She was whispering.

"We've had an attempted break in here and now something very strange is going on in one of our units" she said.

Welcoming the opportunity to get out of the office, Zach said he'd be right there.

When he drove up to the front gate he recognized two of the three members of the welcoming party: the old lady who managed the place and the little queen he'd interrogated. There was a third person: a rather elderly and dignified looking man in a track suit.

As soon as he was out of the car the little queen was at his side, babbling about break-ins, cults, witchcraft and Charles Manson. After a few seconds he got him calmed down and was briefed by Cora. Clearly, something suspicious was going on in one of the condos.

Before heading there he asked who the elderly man was, while extending his hand. The little queen said: "This is my husband, John", all the while smirking. Zach nearly withdrew his hand in shock.

The old guy looked so normal. Even dignified. How could he be "married" to the little old queer? Before he could dwell on this further, the manager was leading them into the compound towards the pool where the body was found.

Although clear, it was a very dark night. The sky was moonless. High above in the palm trees a crow cawed. A gentle breeze caused the trees to rustle and pushed the hot night air against Zach's cheeks. Suddenly, the manager stopped and held up her hand for the rest of them to do likewise. She held her finger to her lips for silence. Then he heard it. A sharp crack followed by a high pitched, but short, scream. They moved closer to the sound. It was coming from behind one of the high walls that surrounded all of the patios. When they got to the front gate Zach peered through. All he could see was red light from within the condo and a shadowy figure moving about. Then he heard the noise again. This time, instead of a scream, the crack was followed by a moan and some indistinguishable words.

Zach wasn't sure what to do. On the one hand, he knew he shouldn't enter private premises without a warrant. On the other, if a crime was in progress and he could thwart it, he did have the right to enter. He tried the gate handle and, to his surprise, found it was unlocked. Following his lead, the little band tiptoed across the patio towards the door. Zach paused and signalled for everyone to be silent…this was unnecessary. There was another loud crack followed by a yelp. Zach pulled his revolver which briefly stuck in its holster.

"This is the Palm Springs Police. Open up!"

There was complete silence.

"I'm giving you a count to five to open this door and then I'm coming in."

He counted down.

Still no response from inside. Zach crooked his right leg and drove his heel into the door. The ancient frame pulled out of the dry plaster and the door fell inwards to the floor. He moved a few feet in, holding his gun in front of him. Then he froze. Facing him was a scene right out of the pictures of Hell in his illustrated Book of Mormon.

An overweight man was tied to two heavy cross beams that formed a kind of sideways cross. He was spread eagled and mostly naked. Around his waist was what looked like the dress a ballerina would wear and his large bottom protruded from under it. It was streaked with marks, some that were bleeding. His shoulders were covered with what looked like melted wax, a possibility that was supported by dozens of lit candles all over the room. The room was bathed in red light that changed shades as the lamp rotated mechanically in front of the bulbs.

There was movement to his right. He turned and found himself facing the devil Himself. A figure draped in blood red robes, with a mask with horns covering its head was moving towards him. It held a threatening cat of nine tails. Zach pointed his gun noticing, as he did, that his hand was shaking. Suddenly the room was fully lit as Cora hit the light switch. The creature in red pulled off its mask. It was Susan.

Zach turned to look behind him. The manager, the little queer and the old guy were frozen, peering through the door. The queer's kimono had fallen open to expose a purple thong. His mouth hung wide and his eyes seemed about to explode. The dignified old guy clung to his companion's arm as if his life depended on it. The manager was clearly struggling to suppress a fit of giggles.

"What the hell are you doing breaking into our house like this?" Susan exploded. She was addressing the three intruders at the door as much as Zach.

"I'm going to sue your fucking asses off" she bellowed. An unfortunate turn of phrase given that Mat's rather large ass was, at that moment, the centre of the tableau.

She advanced menacingly towards the door, waving the whip furiously. Cora, John and I beat a hasty retreat into the darkness of the patio. I fumbled with the gate, all the while expecting this banshee to descend upon us. Eventually I figured that, just like every other gate in the complex, this one opened outwards. It opened and we fled.

Meanwhile, back in the living room, Zach was discovering new words for "I'm so sorry". By now, Mat was bellowing too although, given his state and position, he wasn't exactly threatening. Zach quietly holstered his revolver. He said, "I'm so sorry" one last time and beat a retreat through the patio.

The garden was completely silent with no sign of his fellow adventurers. He considered banging on their doors but thought better of it and returned to the station. He had no idea what to put in his incident report and couldn't even begin to think what shit would hit the fan now.

10

It took almost no time at all for the shit to hit the proverbial fan. John and I were having our regular coffee by the pool the next morning when I spotted Mat heading in our direction. His neck had disappeared as his head rose directly from his shoulders and was thrust forward like a battering ram. His bloodshot gnat eyes were filled with rage. In fact, it looked like he was about to kill someone, probably me. As he bore down on us I calculated the best escape route. The challenge was John who couldn't move very fast anymore. I wondered how it would look if I just fled. I mean Mat wouldn't hurt an old man, would he?

"Listen you pair of fucking old queers, I'm going to sue you for all you're worth. And that's after I get through with the fucking City of Palm Springs and this fucking complex." I felt he had a rather limited vocabulary this morning.

His face was an unnatural colour, something between purple and pink, but with a hint of fuchsia...I couldn't help myself. John sat silent and unmoving.

"Now Mat, I understand why you're angry but, really, all we were doing was trying to help. We heard strange noises coming from your unit and assumed you and Sandy might be in some kind of trouble."

Despite a herculean effort not to, I smirked and let out a little snort although I did try to hide it as a cough. This enraged Mat even more and he advanced menacingly towards me. I was completely in his shadow and certain he was going to strike me. He raised both arms and clenched his fists. He used more bad language. Then he went strangely silent. A look of distress crossed his face. The next thing I knew he tumbled backwards into the deep end of the pool. We sat in stunned silence for a second as he flailed around in the water. Then I sprang into action, jumping up and grabbing the pool cleaning pole. I swung it towards him with all my might. It was surprisingly pliant and delivered a sharp smack across his bobbing head. He gave me a dazed, slightly hurt look and sunk beneath the water. I would have jumped in but I can barely swim and, besides, I have a heart condition. I grabbed one of the floating noodles and threw it at the point where he had disappeared. It landed several feet short. I shouted for help.

By the time Mat's water logged body was dragged from the pool several neighbours had gathered to watch the emergency workers. They made an effort to resuscitate him but, after twenty minutes submerged, to no avail. I couldn't help noticing, as they pulled him from the water, that his sweat pants came partly down exposing his large and lacerated bottom. There was also a welt across his forehead.

I hoped the only witness to Mat's last minutes on this earth was John. Otherwise, someone might think the smack on the head had something to do with his death and that would mean I could be charged with...what? There were lots of windows looking out to the pool and anyone could have been watching, or even listening. He had shouted at us, threatened us, was about to hit me and then he fell into the pool. Might someone conclude that I hit him with the pole in an attempt to drown him? Oh my god! Life in a U.S. penitentiary. Or worse. And what would happen to John? I needed to calm down and act like the almost hero I actually was.

****

Jeffery was barely awake when he heard the commotion out by the pool. He struggled out of bed and parted the blinds. Sunlight initially blinded him but, as his eyes adjusted he saw the source of the noise. Over by the pool a large, dark haired man was in some kind of confrontation with a wiry little guy in a faded kimono. He recognized them both as owners in the complex. He couldn't quite make out who was doing what as the larger guy was standing between him and the little guy and waving his fists in the air. Then he seemed to be pushed backwards into the pool. The little guy grabbed the pool cleaning pole, swung it wide and delivered a vicious blow to his head.

Although he didn't want to get involved, Jeffery felt he had to do something so he dialled 911. When asked, he refused to provide information about himself, describing instead what he had just witnessed and then hanging up.

****

Zach was reviewing the 911 calls from the last twenty four hours when his eyes lit upon one concerning Caballeros Estates. Another death? This one by drowning but with some questions? He logged into the record and looked at the bare details.

Deceased: a mid fifties married guy from LA who also lived at Caballeros Estates with his wife.

Witnesses: the two old queens, one of whom he had interviewed concerning the murder.

Source of 911 call: not given but traced to a landline in the complex.

Likely cause of death: drowning but in broad daylight with others present???

And there were two other details: signs of severe trauma on the deceased's buttocks and a blunt trauma mark across his forehead. Zach let out a low whistle as several possibilities occurred to him. He copied the report and walked it over to Mike's desk.

"Have you seen this?"

Mike did a quick look and then paused halfway down the sheet.

"Holy shit! Could this be a coincidence? I think we'd better track down the person who made that 911 call and pay him a visit."

11

I was naked and pinned down. Two giants pressed my arms to the bed while two others sat on my feet. Their massive arms were covered with amateur tattoos and they stank of cigarettes, dried sweat, testosterone and spent semen. The door to my cell was filled with faces, all shouting encouragement to my assailants. The room was damp and cold with a lingering smell of old urine. I jerked my head to the left and saw my worst nightmare: a giant, naked black man coming at me with his member fully erect and a huge smile on his face. I started to scream but a dirty rag was quickly stuffed in my mouth. I was going to be raped. It was a flashback from "Fortune and Men's Eyes" and I remembered how badly that one ended.

There was knocking. My attackers didn't seem to hear it. More knocking, this time louder and more insistent. Something odd was happening. The knocking was coming from somewhere other than this cell. Consciousness gained the upper hand as I realized the knocking had nothing to do with my dream. Someone was at our back door.

I pulled on my kimono as quietly as possible so as not to wake John whose snores continued to punctuate the night. It was nearly midnight. Who the hell would be banging on the door at this hour? I expected some drunk, or worse so only opened the inner door, leaving the security screen between me and the intruders. I was facing three policemen, including the young punk who interviewed me.

"Sorry to bother you at this time of night Mr Pickle but I'm afraid we have some questions we need answered urgently. May we come in?" One of the older cops asked.

"Well, I, I don't know. It's very late and we're sleeping." I answered. Zach noted his anxious tone.

"I would rather we did this in a cooperative manner Mr Pickle but, if you prefer, we can put it on a much more formal basis."

I gathered the kimono up against my throat and considered my options. There weren't any.

"Well, ok. But please be quiet my husband's sleeping". I detected a slight sneer exchanged between the cops.

As I led them into the living room I noticed the latest copy of Rent Boys lying open on the coffee table. It was too late to get to it and as I sat down I grimaced at the naked policeman with the enormous erection staring up at us all. All he had on was his hat, revolver and boots The other policemen did their best to ignore it but the young kid stared at it with a look of horror, disgust and interest.

"Mr Pickle we are here concerning the drowning two days ago. I believe you were present when it occurred?"

"That's right. One minute Mat was talking to us and the next he was in the pool."

"You say "we", who else was there?"

"My husband." The older officer was asking the questions and didn't seem at all nonplussed by the statement but, again, I was sure I detected a sneer on the young punk's face.

"Was there any one else present?"

"No."

"Well, actually we have located another witness: the person who made the 911 call."

What felt like an electric jolt raced through my body and cold sweat ran down my back. I shivered.

Zach noticed that the little fag paled and his eyes dilated. They darted from Mike to Zach to the magazine on the coffee table that Zach was trying very hard not to notice. He knew there was a naked guy pretending to be a cop on the page and that he had a boner. Little in Zach's past had prepared him for this. Oh, he remembered Granny Smith telling him about the evil of men sleeping with men and promising they would all burn in hell. But to be confronted with it in this way was much, much more troubling. This aging little queen was probably jerking off to the picture while the old guy he lived with slept in the next room. The depths of the depravity disgusted him.

"Good". I winced at the high, reedy sound that came out of my mouth. "Who was that?"

"We're not in a position to release that information to you just yet but you should know that he says you were having an argument with the deceased, there was a bit of a scuffle and then he fell in the pool."

I was aghast. "No such thing happened. We were just having our regular morning coffee by the pool when Mat came over to exchange pleasantries and had some kind of a seizure and fell into the pool."

"Did you do anything to help him when he fell in the pool?"

"Well, I threw a noodle towards him to help him float and I called for help?"

"Noodle?"

"Oh, you know, those foam flotation thingies."

"Nothing more?"

The noose was tightening. My eyes were bulging and I was flushing.

"There was nothing more I could do. I don't swim and he was in the deep end".

"So, you didn't take the cleaning pole and hit him over the head with it?"

I froze. I looked to the left and to the right hoping for some escape. I shook my head to end the nightmare. Finally, I focussed on the coffee table only to be confronted by the naked cop with the big dick. The line between consciousness and unconsciousness had completely blurred and what had been my rather interesting dream now had all the trappings of a full blown nightmare.

"Oh, I forgot. I did try to help him with that pole. Unfortunately, by the time I got it he had sunk beneath the surface. You know, Mat was a very large man."

"What would you say if I told you we have an eyewitness who says you used the pole to hit him when he was very much above the surface and struggling?"

"I would say that person was not telling the truth or, at best, didn't understand what he or she saw."

"Well, Mr Pickle, that about does it for now. Sorry to have intruded into your sleep. However, I'm going to have to ask you to surrender your passport."

I knew what this meant. I was a suspect. Probably the only suspect in a murder investigation. They were afraid I would flee back to Canada or some other place. My carefully constructed life as a retired, gentle gay man was crashing down around me.

"How long will you need it?"

"Until we decide whether there is anything else we need from you." Mike took the passport and handed it to Zach who slipped it into his pocket.

"You'll be hearing from us. G'night." The three cops put their hats back on, touched their brims in some idiotic gesture of politeness and exited.

A cold chill swept over me. I was actually a suspect in a murder case. What would happen to me? Did they still have the death penalty in California? Would it be lethal injection where one drug paralyzes while the other suffocates. Or do they still use the electric chair? Or maybe the gallows?

Even if they don't have the death penalty, how would a delicate creature like me survive in a federal prison surrounded by violent men who are deprived of the company of women?

A panic attack started and I headed for the medicine cabinet to get a Xanax.

****

Things moved quickly after the visit. At ten o'clock the next morning two squad cars pulled up to Caballeros Estates and four policemen came to my door, guns drawn. I nearly fainted.

The older cop from last night did the talking: "Beverly Pickle, I am arresting you for the murder of Mathew Jones. You have the right to remain...."

I could hear the words he was reciting echoing from countless cop shows. I could see the guns pointed at me and the four grim faces. But mostly it was a dream, or should I say a nightmare, one I expected to snap out of at any moment. Only I didn't. Someone grabbed my arm rather roughly, spun me around and pinned me against a wall. I cried out but to no avail as the handcuffs snapped tightly onto my wrists and I was pushed out the door towards the waiting cars. Neighbours were standing by the police cars and staring at me. I couldn't remember where John was. A hand was placed on top of my head and I was shoved into the back of one of the cars, the door slammed and locked. As we moved away from Caballeros Estates my old life passed by and disappeared in the distance.

A siren is a very odd sound when you're in the car sounding it. You hear it, but not exactly. I couldn't distinguish between it and the shrill scream of terror that was ricocheting off the insides of my skull.

This was why Zach became a cop: taking down perps like this degenerate. He checked the rear view mirror as they roared down Arenas, sirens blaring. The little queer looked totally panicked. All the bravado and bullshit about his rights and husband blown right out of him. Zach felt especially virtuous as they passed the little church on the corner. This really was God's work.

After what seemed like hours we pulled into the driveway of a nondescript, single storey building. There was a sign, something to do with police.

12

The case against the suspect seemed pretty straight forward. But there were a number of unanswered questions. First, the lacerations on the victim's buttocks. It almost seemed as if he'd been tortured, although in a very odd way. Then there was the matter of motive. As best he could tell, there wasn't one. Given the recent history of this complex, however, Mike wasn't ruling anything out. The victim was straight and married. So what was the connection with the old gay guy? And how good was the witness? When they'd interviewed him Mike felt something, probably booze and drugs, had damaged the guy's brain. Also, there was the matter of the earlier drug issues and the hotel he once owned. Although he hadn't been convicted of anything, his partner certainly had. And was there some connection between this death and the earlier murder? Work sure had become interesting lately.

****

Zach was torn. On the one hand, he knew he could explain the lacerations on the victim's buttocks but, on the other, doing so would expose his own role in the whole sorry episode the night before, not to mention the slightly incorrect incident report he had filed on it. And the marks didn't seem that important in the greater scheme of things. Although the little queer's presence the night before might be relevant to what happened in the morning. But that would only shift blame to the victim. He was the one with reason to be angry. And that might lead to a claim of self defence. Based on the witness, that didn't seem a likely scenario. How could self defence involve clubbing a drowning man? He also had trouble shaking the image of the naked policeman on the guy's table. Pickle was obviously a serious deviant and, whether or not he meant to kill the guy, everyone would be better with him off the street.

****

Cora was floored when John told her about Beverly's arrest for Mat's murder. In fact, she just didn't believe it. It was bad enough dealing with Mat's death but now, Beverly...a murderer? Ridiculous. I mean, yes, he could be very nasty in an old fashioned gay kind of way. And yes, he spread gossip that was better left unrepeated. And, yes he was so cheap he still owned his first dollar. But a killer? Surely not. And yet the police claimed they had a witness, although they wouldn't say who it was.

****

Susan looked despondently at the empty vodka bottle on the coffee table. If she ever needed a drink, it was now. Instead, she was struggling to absorb the words the cop had just shared with her while experiencing the first hints of the aching return of sobriety. Beverly murdered Mat. Little, old, queenie Beverly? It didn't seem possible. Then she remembered the scene from two nights previous. Beverly was there with the cop and meddling Cora. But how could that have ended up with him killing Mat? According to the police, he pushed Mat into the pool and then smashed him over the head with the cleaning pole. Her big, virile, straight Mat...pushed into the pool by Beverly?? Unbelievable! And yet the police said there was a witness.

Susan wished she'd remained friends with at least a few of the neighbours so she could borrow some vodka right now but that wasn't the case so she went to the fridge, removed half a bottle of old cooking wine and started drinking directly from the bottle.

13

The interview with the cops unsettled Jeffery. It awakened painful memories. As soon as they left he mixed a dry gin martini, went out on the patio and lit a joint. Although he'd seen the people around the complex, he didn't know anything about them and certainly couldn't provide information on an argument or fight. He only went to the pool after midnight and took no part in the social activities at the complex. He called 911 because someone was drowning, not to be a witness in a murder investigation.

At first he didn't hear the phone ringing over the opening chords of "Tristan and Isolde". When he finally reached it all he heard was a dial tone. The list of missed calls showed the number was blocked. He returned to the patio and turned up the music. The phone rang again and this time he picked up on the third ring.

"Hello?" There was no response. "Hello?" Again, no response. He heard breathing and the twang of country music in the background. "Who is this?" No response. "Listen, if this is a wrong number, fine but otherwise, go fuck yourself." He hung up.

Two days later Jeffery opened his mail box to find a heavily wrapped package jammed into it. His name was printed in large, crude letters and there was no return address. He took the package to his condo and opened it. All he found inside was shredded newspaper but, just as he was about to put it aside, a small, hard object wrapped in more newspaper fell to the floor.

A message was scrawled in red ink on the newspaper . It said simply: "Leave Town or Die". Inside was a six inch high GI Joe doll, it's colouring badly faded and its lower body covered with what looked like teeth marks. Jeffery recognized the teeth marks. He was transported back to another time and place. His big bear of a father picking him up and whirling him around, his slightly musky male scent interspersed with sweat, tobacco and alcohol. Then later, cowering in the corner, chewing on the little doll as his mother and father fought, first screaming at each other, then throwing things and then his father punching her. Later still, watching in terror as his father tried to strangle her, rushing to her defence and being thrown in a crumpled and damaged heap against the radiator.

A shudder ran down his spine. He had banished those memories and yet, with this single reminder, they came flooding back.

Where did this come from? Who would send it? And who wanted him to leave town or die?

He hadn't seen the toy in decades. In fact, he hadn't even thought about it in decades. It was one of the few things his long forgotten father gave him somewhere back there in Vegas. Way back there when he was a little boy. He turned it slowly in his hands, trying to calm the nightmare memories it had awakened.

He had to get out of the house. Grabbing his car keys, he headed to the garage. His battered old, red Porsche Targa was sitting in its usual place covered in dust. Jeffery got in, backed out and drove to Arenas Street and the so called "gay village". A black pickup truck with shaded windows and Nevada plates cruised slowly by him going in the other direction.

Jeffery pulled into one of the vacant parking spaces in front of Sidebar. He paused before getting out of the car. It was late on a Wednesday afternoon and the sun was just beginning to set behind the mountains. The street was mostly empty with only a few men hurrying through the heat to reach the air conditioned oases of the bars. Raucous noise was coming from the patio two doors down.

The usual denizens of Sidebar's patio were beginning to wind down the red umbrellas. Although he hadn't been here in months, Jeffery recognized most of the tired, old faces, each one fiercely defending his little piece of the small patio while dragging on an endless stream of cigarettes. A couple of young men sat by themselves in one corner, almost certainly tourists.

As he pushed open the door Jeffery was assaulted by a blast of cold air and the deafening blare of music. He never understood why a bar that was mostly populated by seniors would play music at a level that made it impossible for younger men to have conversations, let alone seniors. His entrance didn't go unnoticed. The ancient "boys" at the bar nudged each other and turned slowly to look in his direction. For a second, he was desirable, just like in the old days. This was the last place on earth where Jeffery was still "chicken".

The loud woman with the garish wig and big glasses was setting up for her weekly show. Hovering nearby was a familiar face, an old drag queen who had been around Palm Springs since before Liberace. He wasn't in drag now and his ancient but unlined face had a strangely boyish quality, something of a cross between a young Truman Capote and a sensitive simian.

In one corner sat a pile of skin and bones, topped by an ancient face underneath a purple Mohawk. He could have leapt off the screen from a George Lucas movie but, then, the bar itself was a geriatric version of the bar in Star Wars. At any moment an ancient Princess Leia could emerge from the washroom determinately pushing a walker.

"What will you have today Jeffery? We have Grey Goose on special". Jeffery looked up at the handsome young bartender. He had a slight recollection of one night at Innsext in the steam room. Had it ended badly? There were so many such memories that he really had no idea.

"Grey Goose, rocks and lime would be good." He smiled and the young guy smiled back.

"Haven't seen you for awhile. Where you been hiding?"

"Oh, just giving the liver a rest."

"Don't you live at Caballeros Estates where that murder happened?"

"I do and here's some more news. It's happened again."

"Huh?"

"A murder. Another murder. This time one of the gay guys living there is the prime suspect. He's a Canadian. You'd recognize him. He comes here sometimes…usually looking for a deal on a glass of white wine. Actually, I'm a witness."

He had the bar tender's full attention.

"Jeffery, over here." He turned and saw his old friend Jerry nursing a drink in a corner of the room. By the number of empty glasses on the table, it appeared he'd been at it for a while. Jeffery took his drink and made his way over to Jerry who was the person he'd come to talk to.

Jerry had aged visibly in the months since he'd last seen him. He was always florid but now the veins on his bulbous nose had sprouted tiny crepuscular tributaries that crept towards his face which itself already bore the telltale signs of a serious drinker. His eyes were rheumy and perpetually tearing. He'd put on a lot of weight and his stomach sat awkwardly and somewhat independently on a stool placed by the banquette. His spindly, white legs protruded from stained khaki shorts that were riding up his thigh to expose flesh the colour and texture of stale cottage cheese.

"So how you been?" he shouted as Jeffery approached. "We've missed you. Wondered if you'd died or something."

Jeffery set his drink on the table and sat on the banquette, careful not to disrupt the stool supporting the stomach.

Jerry was a retired cop from Chicago. To hear him tell it his illustrious career there was cut short when he was outed as gay. There were rumours of a different story though, rumours that said Jerry was involved in a kickback scheme and was lucky to get out with just a termination and reprimand. He'd fled to Palm Springs and settled in a trailer park on the edge of town.

In earlier days, Jerry was a regular guest at Innsext and Jeffery remembered him leaving his door slightly ajar with his blinds open as he lay on the bed naked watching porn on the TV. Now he spent his days at Sidebar, showing up before lunch and then being poured into his car by one of the bartenders in the early evening.

"I need to talk to someone with experience in crime and the law."

Jerry's rheumy eyes focussed and he twitched slightly at the hint of his involvement with crime.

Jeffery described his role in the unfolding murder investigation at Caballeros Estates, followed by the battered toy from his childhood and the threat.

"Do you think I should tell the police?"

Given Jerry's experience with police he didn't think that was a good idea at all, although his speech was slurred as he tried to give that response. Just as Jeffery was about to reframe the question, their table suffered a jolt as a very old man in a walker tried to push past. There wasn't quite enough room and he snarled something incomprehensible. Before either could respond, the old guy drove the walker against the stool, sending it out from under Jerry's resting stomach. Jerry was holding a mostly full glass of vodka and the sudden shift in his centre of gravity pulled him off the banquette towards the floor, while spilling his drink down his front.

"What the fuck do you think you're doing you old fart?" Jerry was no respecter of age, particularly after a few "beverages".

The old guy ignored him and kept moving towards the door, all the while muttering something in the direction of the floor. Jeffery helped Jerry up. The front of his shirt was soaked and little streams of vodka were dripping from his shorts onto his battered shoes.

"One of these days I'm going to lay that old bugger out flat. He gets nastier and more demented by the day." he shouted as he made his way to the washroom.

Just as Jeffery was settling back onto the seat and trying to get the waiter's attention to wipe up the mess and refill Jerry's drink there was a commotion at the bar. A young man was having a confrontation with the bar tender who was asking him to leave.

"You fucking fags are all the same. Well you can suck my big fat dick."

He turned to leave and his eyes briefly met Jeffery's whose stomach jumped. There was something weirdly familiar about him and yet Jeffery couldn't remember ever having seen him before. The guy, actually no more than a kid, definitely had something wrong with him but why did he look so familiar? His eyes weren't quite aligned and had a completely vacant look and his head bounced with a slight tremble like a hanging car ornament. He pushed several men out of his way, stormed out the door and was gone.

Jeffery had had enough of Sidebar. He just wanted to go home. He didn't wait for Jerry to return as he left out the back door.

14

I hadn't slept a wink. It was strange lying in bed alone. John returned to Canada, his annual time allowance for a Canadian to stay in the States up. And here I am, alone and afraid in this purgatory. It seems like decades since this was our desert oasis, free from worries, pressures or threats. Now it's a prison. Literally. A prison.

Cora found me a lawyer. He's a very pushy, overweight faggot who bills by the nanosecond and whose reedy voice puts my teeth on edge. Our first meeting didn't go well. There I was, frightened and vulnerable, in need of comfort and reassurance and what did I get? He walked into his oh so chic desert minimalist reception area clad in white Bermuda shorts and a soft pink polo shirt, all on top of expensive alligator loafers that he wore without socks. His gay receptionist, whose name was Lance of course, reeked of cologne and introduced me in an irritating, lisp infused staccato. The lawyer barely nodded as he signalled me to follow him.

Things got worse once we were in his office. Instead of waiting to hear my concerns, he cut me off and spoke as if I was a child. Each time I tried to ask a question he put his hand up, palm first, signalling for silence. I mean, who was the client and who was the lawyer here? The more he spoke, the less confidence I had but there was really no alternative. I knew no other lawyer in town, nor anyone who could recommend one. Also, there was the not so small matter of money. These guys were bandits! When I arrived at the office, the first thing the receptionist did was charge a $10,000 retainer to my credit card. This was the price of admission.

Despite my reservations, he did get me bail, something that seemed unlikely given the nature of the charges. We used all our savings and mortgaged our home to get a bond bailsman to lend us the money. And it was made clear that if I skipped they would come after me no matter where I fled. Probably with some bounty hunter like that monstrous looking creature on TV. In any case, I surrendered my passport and agreed to wear an ankle bracelet that emitted a signal if I left the geographic boundaries of Palm Springs. I couldn't even go to Trader Joe's or El Paseo. This really was prison.

That said, the real prison was much worse. Just thinking about it makes me ill. I was stuck there for three days placed in a holding cell with some extraordinarily unpleasant and unclean people. One of them even picked on me. Said something about wanting my pussy. I was terrified. They finally transferred me to a single holding cell but, really, that wasn't much better. Food shoved through the door. A slot opened every few hours to check on me. As if there was anything to check on. What was I going to do? Where was I going to go? Maybe they thought I was a suicide risk…admittedly the thought did occur to me in the bleakest moments…but, again, how? I had no belt. No sharp tools. No pills. Anyway, I'm much too much of a coward to do anything like that. And besides I'm totally innocent.

The court appearance wasn't what I expected. The visitors' gallery was packed. Cora was there with a couple of my neighbours. So was Susan, dressed completely in black, milking the role of grieving widow. She glared at me malevolently through her veil as I entered the courtroom. There was no doubt what her verdict was.

The area set aside for press was packed, this being the biggest trial to hit Palm Springs in decades. As well as the Desert Sun and the local radio and TV stations, papers from LA, San Diego, Phoenix and Vancouver sent reporters. I was famous for all the wrong reasons.

The judge was a woman. A very large, black woman with heavy glasses and a voice right out of "Good Times". When she directed me to stand and enter my plea, for some completely inexplicable reason I felt terribly guilty. I planned to say "not guilty your Honour" with composure and self assurance but I was barely able to squeak "not guilty".

The prosecutor opposed bail and, for a while, I thought I was going to spend the next several months incarcerated. I would have expired. Finally, after seemingly endless arguments back and forth between my lawyer and the prosecutor, the judge granted bail but with very onerous conditions. One million dollars! And then there was the ankle bracelet condition. I was so relieved I gave little thought to what that would mean.

So, I'm required to wear an ankle bracelet in broiling Palm Springs. And not one you'd mistake for a fashion accessory. It's waterproof but the first time I went to the pool with it, all conversation stopped and everyone stared at the black band around my ankle. I was marked as a murderer.

Even going to a bar or restaurant is difficult. At this time of year, shorts are de rigueur but that leaves the little accessory exposed. I tried wearing socks to cover it and ended up looking geeky… and not in a good way. Now, I mostly eat pizza at home and pray for a miracle.

I heard a loud bump right above my bedroom. That's strange. It's the middle of the night and that apartment's been empty since Adele's murder. I held my breath and listened. Another bump and the sound of footsteps.

I got out of bed, put on my kimono and quietly opened the door to the patio. Adele's patio overlooked ours and by moving to the far side I hoped I could get a view of who was up there. It was pitch black but, in any case, the ledge blocked a clear view of her living room. I pulled one of my patio chairs over. It's very cheap but was given to me by a neighbour when he was upgrading from Wal-Mart to Target. It was on coasters and rotated but I managed to steady it by placing my hand against the wall. Shadows were moving about Adele's living room. I stretched upwards. Suddenly the chair did a forty five degree rotation and lurched forward several inches. I lost contact with the wall and tumbled towards the rest of the patio furniture while emitting a little shriek. When I hit the glass table top it crashed onto the hard tiles and broke into thousands of tiny pieces. I landed on them.

It took what seemed like hours for the shock to wear off although, in retrospect, I suspect it was seconds. Something warm was running down the hand that had broken my fall. Then I heard footsteps up above. Someone was moving towards me. I stopped breathing.

The moon was mostly covered by cloud and my patio was in complete darkness. By lying very still I hoped to be invisible. The footsteps got closer. Then they stopped. A shadow appeared at the edge of the upper patio. It was motionless but the more I looked, the more it took form as a man's silhouette. He was staring straight at me. That's when I noticed with horror the tiny red light blinking from the little accessory. I leapt to my feet and raced into the house, slamming and locking the door behind me.

Something was dragged across the floor upstairs. Footsteps descended the stairs by my door. I tested the lock. They got very close, then receded.

I turned on the light and looked in horror at my hands and robe. They were covered in blood as if I had just participated in some kind of murderous ritual.

15

Zach was finishing his notes on the interrogation of the little queen from Caballeros Estates when he was called to the switchboard. A distraught woman from the condo complex across from the Catholic church on Arenas was on the phone. He had trouble making sense of what she was saying but it was something about a smell, a dog and a body. No other officers were in the office on the hot Sunday afternoon and, instead of calling for help, Zach decided to check out the complaint himself.

There was a small welcoming party waiting as he pulled up in front of the complex. One, particularly sensible looking woman stepped forward as soon as he got out of the car. Her name was Inez and it was her partner who called the police. Their condo overlooked a vacant lot immediately east of the complex. An increasingly unpleasant smell had been coming from the lot over the past few days. Shortly after lunch their Cockapoo, Ella, escaped out the front door and they found her sniffing a decomposing body behind sage brush on the vacant lot. It was the source of a now unbearable stench. Inez offered to lead Zach to the body.

The correct thing for Zach to do was to call for backup but he didn't want to appear green so, without communicating back to the station, he followed Inez as she strode purposefully into the deserted lot. Several residents of the complex followed a few feet behind. A sweet, sickly smell increased with each step. Had he been more experienced, Zach would have recognized that smell. The buzzing of excited insects grew louder as they approached. And then there it was: the body of a woman lying face up, her eyes frozen in a look of surprise. Inez pointed to a gaping indentation on the left side of her head that was covered in congealed, black blood swarming with maggots. Her teeth were bared in a macabre rictus. Two of them were missing. Her skirts were pulled up and a broken piece of cactus was jammed between her legs.

The low hum of flies. The oozing black blood and maggots. The sickening stench of death. The relentless, beating sun. Zach felt dizzy. He closed his eyes and took a deep breath. A wave of nausea swept over him. Before he could stop it, vomit spewed from his mouth. He fell to his knees as heaves wracked his body. Inez looked on contemptuously from a few feet away.

****

Even though it was his day off, Mike took the call. It was from the kid Zach and he assumed it had something to do with the murder at Caballeros Estates. To his surprise, a woman's voice responded to his greeting. Inez was using Zach's phone as he was apparently indisposed.

Mike's day off was ruined. He had a squad car at the house and got to the crime scene in minutes. It was a scorching day and the people on the sidewalk were huddled under a small patch of shade from an adjacent tree. He saw another squad car, this one with someone slumped over the wheel. A heavy set woman was waving at him. As he approached he saw it was Zach in the car, his head face down on the steering wheel. The woman introduced herself as Inez and explained that Zach had keeled over at the sight of the body. Mike took one look at the kid and then followed her into the vacant lot.

The onlookers moved from the protection of the shade to get a closer look. As he followed Inez Mike recognized the smell of a decomposing corpse. They rounded a clump of sagebrush and there it was. It was the homeless woman from the church. Her body was twisted around a small outcropping of rock, her head forced back revealing a giant black dent on the side. Her multiple skirts were pulled up and a piece of cactus protruded from between her legs. The stench was overwhelming and they retreated a few feet up wind. Mike was already calling for reinforcements and a van from the coroner's office when Zach appeared looking as if he had seen a ghost. A thin green line of vomit ran down his chin and settled on his uniform.

16

The morning followed its monotonous routine. First, Luis took the leaf blower and walked around the compound blowing leaves and other refuse from the pathways, beds and lawns. Then he went around again with the cart, sweeping everything up and loading it into the garbage bin. After that, he pruned one of the orange trees that was getting out of shape and mowed the lawn fronting the complex on Avenida Caballeros.

It was Friday and he could hardly wait for it to end. His friend, Miguel was driving him to the immigration detention centre south of San Diego in the morning. It was his first visit with Chita since she was snatched away by the immigration authorities. There was no way to prevent her deportation. All that could happen is a delay. And for what? She was in prison and would be better off in Mexico. He considered whether or not to go back to Mexico with her. But he'd worked so hard for his green card and his family depended on the money he sent back each month. He was trapped between his love for Chita and the other obligations.

He was moving by a rather unkempt flower bed behind the large Jacuzzi when something caught his eye. Something glittered. He walked over to see what it was. Lying partly hidden under the lower leaves of a Bird of Paradise was a ladies' handbag. The sun's rays glinted off its metal clasp. He picked it up, turned it over a couple of times and tried the clasp. It opened to reveal a compact, some lipstick, a tissue and a large bundle of hundred dollar bills.

Luis knew he should give the handbag and its contents to Cora but something, perhaps the possibility of a reward, made him hold back and, instead he took it to the little room where he stored his personal belongings and placed it behind a cupboard.

The hidden purse weighed heavily on Luis the next day as they drove towards San Diego but as they drew closer other concerns moved to the fore. The approach to the immigration holding facility was intimidating. As they passed through multiple layers of security Luis worried they wouldn't be let back out. He felt suspicion and hostility from the gringos asking questions at each stop. Finally they were directed into a parking lot where their truck joined many other dilapidated vehicles. Luis left Miguel in the truck, gripped his green card tightly in his pocket and went to a window where everyone was being screened before being admitted. In front of him were whole families laden with food and drink. He worried that he hadn't brought a gift for Chita but it hadn't occurred to him in the rush to get ready. Much to his relief the woman at the window gave him barely a look as she buzzed him in.

Inside, a Spanish speaking woman asked for details of his visit and then directed him down a long, non descript corridor to a windowless room where reunions where already underway. There was crying and singing and excited chatter in Spanish. As directed, he took a seat and waited. The door opposite opened and closed admitting prisoners to the room. Finally, it opened and there she was looking tiny, frightened and confused. He started to shout her name but choked. She saw him and a wonderful smile lit up her face. He rushed to her and they embraced.

The hour allocated for the visit passed in an instant. It seemed they had just embraced when a stern looking woman came over and tapped Chita on the shoulder, indicating it was time for her to go back inside.

Luis couldn't get the tearful image of Chita out of his mind as they drove back to Palm Springs. He had to find something, anything, to help her. There must be some way she could stay in America. If only he was a citizen and could sponsor her but, with only a green card, that wasn't an option.

The first thing he did when he got home was call his priest. He recommended that Luis talk to an immigration lawyer and gave him the name of one in Cathedral City. Luis met him after work the next day. The bottom line was it would take money, a lot of money to pursue a legal remedy. In all, the lawyer estimated it would take at least ten thousand dollars, an impossibly large sum for Luis.

Driving home he formed a plan and detoured back to Caballeros Estates. He parked out of sight at the back and went to his storage room. The purse was where he left it. He pulled out the wad of hundred dollar bills and counted them. There was ten thousand dollars. Luis tucked them inside his shirt and went home.

That night Luis wrestled with the devil. On the one hand he knew the money belonged to someone else and he had no right to it. On the other, he thought of the good he could do with it, freeing Chita to join him permanently in America. He considered asking the priest but decided against it, knowing what he would say and not willing to abandon the dream. Finally, at about three in the morning he fell asleep and dreamed that the Virgin Mary came to him and told him to use the money to help Chita. He woke feeling better than he had in months. Luis now understood the money was left there for him, not by its earthly owner but by the Virgin. He drifted back to sleep and dreamed of ravishing Chita.

17

Zach couldn't accept there was no connection between the three homicides. At least two were tied directly to Caballeros Estates and the third was only a few blocks away by the church where the first funeral was held. The suspect in the bludgeoning/drowning was present when the first murder happened but, despite his best efforts, Zach couldn't find any way to link him to it. As for the bag lady's murder, there was absolutely nothing to connect him. And yet…he couldn't let it go. Deep down he knew they had uncovered a homicidal little fairy who, for reasons unknown, was murdering innocent men and women. He asked the Lord for guidance and inspiration.

He pulled up the file on the suspect. New information was added as a result of contact with the Mounties in Canada. On the whole, he looked innocent enough but there were a couple of entries that interested him. First, he'd had two DUI's, although they were eight and eleven years ago. Second, he'd been in a bath house in Toronto when it was raided resulting in a charge of indecent exposure and disorderly conduct. Recently, there were a number of trips to Provincetown and San Diego, all on his own. He'd visited them a combined total of eight times in the last four years. Contacting the police in each of those cities to see if there were any unsolved murders that might be similar to the slayings in Palm Springs was the logical next step.

He called San Diego first where an officious woman pointed out he had the same access as they to the record of unsolved murders in southern California. Eventually, she turned him over to a homicide detective who was more helpful. As it turned out, there were murders in San Diego at the time of each of the little queer's visits and, at least two of them bore a similarity to two of the Palm Springs killings. In one, the victim was found bludgeoned to death in the pool of a hotel known to cater to homosexuals and, in the other, an elderly woman was killed with an axe in her home a few blocks from the area known as the "gay village". Zach's heartbeat quickened as he pulled up the information on both cases and downloaded it.

Then he called Provincetown. There were two murders in P-town during the periods the suspect was in town. One involved a Vietnamese drag queen named Honey Pot who was found floating face down at the foot of the dick dock and the other, an elderly man known to befriend younger, single men visiting town. He died from a blow to the head with a blunt instrument. The drag queen also showed signs of blunt trauma to the head except that by the time she was located various sea animals had had their way with her and, as a result, the exact cause of death could not be determined. Both crimes remained unsolved.

Zach was sure he was on to something. He wondered if there were more victims out there, victims of a homo serial killer. He considered discussing this with Mike but, on reflection knew he needed more evidence to persuade him. Where to begin? Although Pickle was charged with the murder at the pool, they hadn't searched his condo. That seemed a serious oversight and so he applied for a search warrant. Given that Pickle was already a named defendant the application was granted quickly. He took two officers with him and headed for Caballeros Estates.

****

I was awakened from my customary afternoon nap by banging. My sleep mask provided complete darkness and, for a second, I thought it was the middle of the night. I had been dreaming, actually, having a nightmare that involved the electric chair, when the noise intruded. Although I was shirtless, it was hot and I stumbled to the door, opened it and was confronted by my nemesis: the kid cop with attitude.

"What is it now?"

"Mr Pickle, we have a search warrant for your apartment. Would you please open the door."

"What the fuck are you up to now?"

"As I said, we have a search warrant and you can let us in voluntarily or we are authorized to take down this door."

This was a no brainer. I opened the door and stood back as three policemen with cardboard boxes came in. Suddenly I felt naked and headed for the bedroom to find a shirt.

"Don't go in there. In fact, we require you to leave us here alone."

"Well I need a shirt. Come with me and watch if you want." He flinched. I went in the bedroom and put on a shirt. No one followed. When I came out I was aghast at what was happening. My sofa was overturned and all the cushions were unzipped. Drawers were being opened and the contents tossed on the floor. One guy was kneeling down in front of my desktop while removing the hard drive. Before I could say anything the kid told me to leave again. I began to object but realized it was futile. I went out the door and sat on the patio.

The search turned up all sorts of things, things Zach had never seen before, let alone imagined. When they lifted the bed he discovered a large black plastic garbage bag obviously containing something substantial. He picked it up, opened the tie and turned it upside down. Suddenly his feet were engulfed in a terrifying collection of artificial penises. There were large black ones, even larger bright pink ones and one that had ominous ridges all up its shaft. When they hit the floor they bounced gaily about in a macabre choreography before settling in a little pyre of latex around his frozen feet. For a second Zach thought he was having a panic attack. He couldn't breathe or move. Then he noticed the other officers staring at him with undisguised glee. He cleared his throat, kicked his way out of the pile and said "fuckin faggots". That was when he remembered that one of the patrol men helping with the search was gay. He flushed as he tried to eke out "I'm sorry" while moving backwards, only to slip on one of the errant dildoes and tumble backwards banging his head with some force on the tiled floor.

Zach lay there stunned for a few seconds. Three concerned, but still smirking, faces stared down at him. Behind them he could see a perfect reflection of himself in the mirrored ceiling. He raised himself on one arm only to find he was staring directly into the crotch of a male blow up doll that was anatomically correct and was dressed in nothing more than a pair of black chaps. Worst of all, a stack of pornographic magazines was dislodged as he fell and fanned out around him. They depicted every kind of depravity between men he could imagine, as well as some that would never have occurred to him.

There were handcuffs and other types of restraints as well as paddles and whips. There was also a hunting knife and, most interesting of all, a hatchet.

As he tried to rise, Zach knew something was terribly wrong. The room was spinning and wave after wave of nausea swept over him. He barely made it to the bathroom before throwing up.

The gay officer drove him to the Emergency Department at Desert Regional where a doctor confirmed a concussion. Zach was directed to bed rest for the next five days.

The search of the two computers revealed an article from the Provincetown paper about the murder of the drag queen although there was nothing about the other murder in that city.

As Zach reflected on the case from his sick bed he was amazed at what they had found. The guy seemed like a harmless, nelly old queen with a lot of attitude. Instead, this search revealed him to be a seriously sick pervert. And what about the other guy? The old man? Was he somehow involved? That just didn't fit. No, Zach was sure the suspect was the owner of all the disgusting evidence.

18

It was like no sound she had ever heard. Not a scream exactly. More like the death rattle of some alien creature. Candy awoke soaked in sweat and gasping for breath. She had cast the covers aside over night but her T-shirt and panties clung to her like a disgusting film. Early morning light shone through a tear in the nearly sheer curtains illuminating the dingy motel room. A rusting air conditioner under the window wheezed and rattled in a losing battle against the sweltering heat. The lingering stench of cheap perfume and cigarettes hung in the air. Although muted, the TV was on and an unattractive older woman with extravagant blond hair and heavy makeup was waving a bible and mouthing something silently at her from the screen.

Candy's nostrils were clogged and dry and her mouth tasted of stale cigarettes and bourbon. A dull ache settled over her head. She raised herself slowly on one elbow, cleared her throat and spat the yellowy/green phlegm into the full ashtray by the bed.

Then she heard it again. A scream so shocking she sat bolt upright despite the shot of pain that raced across her forehead. What the fuck was happening? She swung her feet over the edge of the bed, vaguely noticing the unmade and empty bed next to hers, stood and moved towards the door.

She opened the door a crack and peered out into the morning light. At first she saw nothing but then detected movement to her right. A few feet down the rusty veranda Jake was standing with his back to her. He was focussed on something in front of him, occasionally poking it and then jumping back and emitting a kind of manic screech. Fortunately, hers was the last room along the veranda and, as far as she could tell, there were no other guests in the adjoining room on the other side. She moved slowly out the door, mindful that she was dressed only in a T-shirt and panties.

"Jake, honey, what are you doing?"

At the sound of her voice he froze. He was wearing a dirty sweat shirt with a hood, sweat pants and battered sneakers that, sometime in the past, had been white. Candy noticed what looked like blood dripping to the floor in front of him.

"Honey, I just heard an awful scream from out here. What was it?"

He seemed to shudder then slowly twisted his torso to partially face her. His eyes, that were not aligned anyway, looked even stranger from this angle. He gave her a kind of loopy grin.

"Nothing momma, nothing."

She moved towards him. He stiffened and made to block her view.

"Come on honey. Let me see."

He grinned sheepishly then moved slightly to one side. Behind him hung a cat in the final stages of dying. It was hung from the railing, split from neck to stomach and its guts were moving slowly towards the floor.

"Oh honey, you shouldn't have done that. Cut it down and clean up this mess before someone sees it."

He looked troubled at her criticism, furrowing his brow and bobbing his head in a kind of rhythmic movement.

"Here, I'll get a wet towel. You cut it down and throw it where no one will find it." She went inside to the bathroom, took one of the worn off-white hand towels, wet it and went back to the porch. Jake had already cut down the dead animal and flung it from the balcony into the desert scrub behind the motel. She wiped up the blood, deposited the dirty towel in a plastic shopping bag and hid it under the trash in the waste basket.

✱✱✱✱✱✱✱✱✱

Candy's life began in a trailer park on the outskirts of Los Vegas. By the time her mother abandoned her at twelve, she had already been in and out of a juvenile detention facility for shoplifting and assault and battery. She liked the company of older men and, at age fourteen was pregnant. Although she wasn't sure, she believed the father was a Mexican nineteen year old she'd been with for several weeks. When she told him he wanted nothing to do with her and denied being the father. She dared not tell her father who, after the disappearance of her mother, grew increasingly violent towards her and her brother. Most of the time he was drunk. If they were lucky he'd pass out before doing too much damage to them.

Candy had a backstreet abortion eight weeks after she found out she was pregnant. The dirty old man that performed it seemed more interested in touching her between her legs than getting rid of the baby. She still shuddered at the memory of his sour breath as his hand worked the metal instrument between her legs. She was lucky. There was no infection and her father didn't notice a thing when she came back to the trailer that night. She paid for the abortion by giving blow jobs to sweaty, drunk tourists in an alley off the Strip.

A few weeks after the abortion Candy noticed a change in her father's behaviour. He'd still come home drunk but, instead of yelling at her, he'd ask that she join him for a beer. At first it seemed weird but Candy soon realized she liked being treated like a grown up. Then the little gifts started. Nothing special or expensive but nice little things like chocolates or costume jewellery. Once, when he brought home some drop earrings he asked her to model them wearing a pair of her mother's high heels. He liked sitting close to her.

All this happened without Mikey seeing it. From an early age, he learned to avoid his father, particularly when he was drunk. He was never around when his father came home, sneaking in much later when everything was quiet and Candy was asleep in the twin bed next to his. Relations between the siblings were strained or nonexistent. They were never close. The four year difference in their ages contributed to that but when Candy came home from school one day and found him parading up and down in front of the mirror dressed in her best dress and shoes she started calling him a faggot. He responded with even more outlandish behaviour. He boasted he had a boyfriend, a much older boyfriend, and he gave him blowjobs that he described in intimate detail. Candy's response was to call him a "fucking faggot" and threaten to "beat the shit out of him" if he ever touched her clothes again.

One night after three beers, her father asked her to sit on his lap. She was a bit tipsy but, even if that weren't the case, would have welcomed the intimacy with an adult. Once she was on his lap, his hand moved slowly up her leg, touching her most private parts. She was thrilled and planted a kiss on his beery mouth. From then on, she looked forward to his return each night, being sure to have makeup and her most adult clothes on. It was only a matter of time before she was giving him blow jobs while he worked his finger into her vagina and played with her breasts. One night he asked her to take off her panties and sit astride him. She did and, despite the pain, felt a thrill as he penetrated her. He didn't notice she wasn't a virgin.

After several weeks of having sex with her father Candy missed her period. She knew from previous experience this was not good. She went to the free medical clinic a few blocks from the trailer park and got the news she was pregnant. Her first impulse was to have another abortion but she had no money to pay for it. She asked her father for the money but he was a devout Catholic and the thought of aborting his child, even one conceived with his daughter, was out of the question. They fought for several weeks. Candy came to hate him and detest his drunken advances.

One Friday night he came home from work already drunk having stopped at a bar along the way. He gave her flowers and then asked that she change into her negligee. She threw the flowers on the floor and refused. At first he tried to reason with her, running his hands up her legs and trying to kiss her. She pushed him away and called him a "fucking pervert". He got angry and rushed towards her. They wrestled into the kitchen where he tried to pin her on the table. She slid free, grabbed the iron frying pan that was sitting dirty in the sink and slammed it with all her might into the back of his head. For a second, time stood still. He looked at her with a kind of bewildered confusion and then reeled backwards, his head hitting the sink before he crumbled to the floor. Blood leaked from his forehead, nose and mouth, first in little trickles and then in torrents. His breaths were accompanied by a gurgling sound. Candy fled to her friend Tammy's home a few trailers down. She pounded on the door and, when it opened, fell in sobbing.

It took a while for Candy to tell Tammy what happened and what led up to it. Candy was sure if she went back, her father would kill her. They weighed their options and decided to go to the trailer together and try to figure out what was happening now by looking through the windows.

While Candy was at Tammy's Mikey came home. As usual, he cased the trailer before going in. Although all the lights were on, there was no movement or sound. At first he assumed his father was boinking Candy in the bedroom. He opened the door as cautiously and quietly as he could. Still no sound. He tiptoed in and headed to his bedroom which was just behind the kitchen. Then he saw it. His father's body. It was lying in a pool of blood that was congealing around a cut on his head. He wasn't breathing. Mikey stood uncertain for a moment. Then, as if a cloud had lifted, he hurried to his room, packed the few things he cared about in an old knapsack and fled.

When Candy and Tammy got to the trailer's kitchen window they found it too high to get a good look in. Tammy gave Candy a boost up so she could take a look. She let out a gasp and said "oh fuck. I think I killed him." They went in through the door and checked the lifeless body. Tammy felt for a pulse. There was none. He was dead.

The girls sat in the living room drinking beer trying to figure out what to do next. Tammy thought they should call the police. Candy wasn't so sure but eventually Tammy prevailed and called 911 which resulted in a squad car pulling into the trailer park a few minutes later.

The investigation into the death took only a few days before it was closed. Candy told the police her father was trying to rape her and she defended herself with the frying pan. This, along with the fact she was already pregnant with his child, persuaded them she was telling the truth and the case was put down to just another domestic brawl between white trash. Her father was buried in an unmarked grave several miles outside the city.

While the police didn't pursue charges, Candy was underage and pregnant and that attracted the attention of the Nevada Child Welfare Department. She was placed in the care of a Catholic charity run by an order of nuns. Even though her pregnancy resulted from rape and incest, an abortion was out of the question. The sisters wouldn't countenance it and, because they feared she might run off and get one, kept her strictly confined during the remainder of her pregnancy. Several months later she gave birth to an underweight baby boy she named Jake.

The moment Candy saw Jake she knew something was terribly wrong with him. For one thing, his left eye was noticeably higher than his right. What was more disturbing was that he didn't cry...really not at all. He just lay there and stared back at her with no noticeable expression on his face. No smile, no frown, no grimace...nothing. The first time she nursed him he bit down so hard she let out a scream. He didn't react, just kept biting and sucking. Eventually, the nuns agreed he should be weaned early and fed formula.

19

In the normal course of things, Jake would have been given up for adoption. That would have satisfied Candy. The problem was no prospective parents wanted him. It took only one look to see he was terribly damaged and any future with him would be difficult and unhappy. Months went by. Candy came to see Jake as a kind of pet. She enjoyed taking him out for walks in a stroller and got particular pleasure from the reaction of strangers as they leaned into the stroller to see him and then reared back in embarrassed shock. It was as if she had a pet reptile and they were expecting a puppy.

Life at the home was increasingly unbearable as the sisters expected her to attend school, take religious instruction, do chores and look after Jake. They steered clear of Jake and some even made the sign of the cross when they passed near him.

One night Candy woke to a gurgling sound from the adjacent crib. She got up, put on the light and looked at Jake. His eyes were wide open and expressionless and a gurgling sound was coming from his mouth. Candy picked him up and walked back and forth in the tiny bedroom. That's when she made her decision. She lay him back in his crib, went to the closet, pulled out the duffel bag used to transfer her belongings from the trailer and filled it with those belongings as well as the few baby supplies that were in the room. She lifted Jake from the crib, wrapped him in a blanket, and carried him and the bag to the hallway. The lights were dim and there was no one around. Candy hurried down the emergency exit stairs and out into the cold desert night. She had a bit of cash and was able to flag a taxi. It took her and Jake to her father's trailer. She didn't have a key but the door was unlocked.

Inside, little had changed from when she left. Dirty dishes were in the sink, now covered in mould. A dark stain marked the linoleum where her father had fallen. There was no sign of Mikey. When she checked his room she saw that his few possessions were gone. She settled Jake on the sofa and began the task of turning the trailer back into a home.

The limits of their Christian charity exhausted with Candy and Jake, the nuns were secretly pleased to be rid of them. They allowed the sin of omission and failed to report their disappearance to anyone. They were just two more missing kids in Vegas and no one cared enough to look for them.

With Mikey gone, Candy was the sole heir to her father's estate and, in time possessed his bank account and trailer. The few thousand dollars in the account allowed her to get the trailer back to a liveable state and to look after Jake for a couple of months. After that she needed to earn a living. Her old friend Tammy showed her how.

Tammy's boyfriend ran a string of hookers. He and his friends stood on the strip and gave out cards with naked photos of the girls to any tourist who would take one. When a connection was made he'd call the girl and she'd go to the john's hotel room. The boyfriend took sixty percent of her take. Sometimes things got out of hand and a girl was beaten up or worse but, usually having the boyfriend know the location of the john's room was enough to provide protection.

Candy fit right in. Although only fifteen, heavy makeup and a certain attitude allowed her to pass as older. Occasionally a john would ask her age and look sceptical when she said "18" but the temptation of young flesh usually triumphed over any concern he might have about statutory rape. Candy made friends with the other girls and some of them even babysat Jake while she was turning a trick. This continued for over three years when, at eighteen she was anxious to move up the Los Vegas food chain.

Although Candy had a slim body men were very attracted to, her breasts were small. She wanted them augmented and one night tricked with a Plastic Surgeon who offered to do them in exchange for sex. Two months later, Candy was showing off a pair of prize breasts while dancing around a pole in a crowded bar.

Getting her breasts done was her first step in moving to a higher rung in the Vegas service industry. Work as a stripper followed. Candy loved the animal attention of the men she stripped for. Sometimes she would let one take her to his hotel room where other favours were provided for cash. For the next several years she mixed stripping and whoring.

As Candy moved through her twenties she sensed her ability to earn a living with her body slipping away. She was now one of the older "girls" and johns were usually looking for their own personal Lolita. She decided to become management. Having learned a lot from her time working the streets it was a relatively easy transition. Now she employed the girls and the Central American men passing out cards on the Strip. She bought a second trailer and set it up as a small whorehouse. It was only fifty feet from her home which allowed her to be both mother and madam simultaneously.

20

Candy nursed a terrible anger towards the mother who abandoned her. She blamed her for all the bad things in her life, whether her father raping her, her multiple pregnancies, her life as a hooker, they were all her mother's fault. Amongst her father's belongings she found a battered brown envelope filled with notes on her mother. He had tried to find her during the first few months after her disappearance. At one point he hired a private detective and it was his notes that revealed the tale of Lucy's life in Palm Springs. There was also a letter from Lucy to Candy's father, apparently in response to one he had sent, that refused his demand for money and told him to never contact her again. It was dated September 4, 1978. After that, nothing. There was an address at the top of the envelope.

As she turned fifty, Candy wanted to break free of her life as a third tier Vegas madam and find another way to support herself and Jake who, at 36, had the brain of a twelve year old. Increasingly she obsessed about her hated mother. As best she could tell from the materials in the old envelope, her mother was living a good life in Palm Springs. Candy felt it her due that she and her son should share in it. She hired her own private detective to update the information from 1978. He located Lucy, now known as Adele and identified her various holdings in Palm Springs.

Candy first attempted to contact Adele by letter. She got no response. Then she tracked down a phone number and called her. As soon as she identified herself, Adele hung up. A second call resulted in Adele telling her to leave her alone or she would contact the police.

Finally, Candy decided she and Jake should pay a visit to their mother and grandmother. They drove to Palm Springs in her black pickup truck.

They checked into a cheap motel just off 111 on the western outskirts of Cathedral City. The private detective met them there and provided Adele's address. He also updated the information on her substantial real estate holdings in and around Palm Springs. This only whetted Candy's appetite.

The private detective also provided some new and unwelcome news. Her long lost brother, Mikey, was not only alive and well but living in Palm Springs in the same complex as their mother. He had assumed a new name and identity and was in a condo owned by Adele. This was very bad news. He was a threat to what Candy now believed was her rightful inheritance. All of this only fuelled her sense of grief against Adele. Not only had she abandoned her to her father's predations, she favoured her brother. She would have to find a way to get him out of the picture.

Candy made another call to Adele and this time would not be put off. When Adele threatened to hang up Candy told her she was in town with her son, Adele's grandson and she knew where Adele lived. After several calls, Adele agreed to give her $10,000 on condition she never bother her again. Candy's initial response was dismissive but then decided it was a good start. She arranged to meet Adele at her home at Caballeros Estates. To avoid the always inquisitive neighbours seeing the transaction, Adele insisted they meet after midnight.

When Candy and Jake pulled up to Caballeros Estates, Adele was waiting at the gate. She carried a small handbag containing $10,000 in cash. She let Jake and Candy into the compound but wouldn't invite them to her condo. When she first saw Jake she was clearly shocked. Not only was he obviously mentally damaged, but he bore an eerie resemblance to her late husband. She guessed he was the father.

At first Jake was very quiet as he stared at this lady who was supposed to be his grandmother. His head bobbed up and down and his hands shook. Adele couldn't bear to look at him and turned her attention to the daughter she hadn't seen in nearly forty years. Candy stood expectantly, waiting for she knew not what. Adele abruptly pushed the purse into Candy's face and told her to get lost and to take Jake with her. She also said she never wanted to see or hear from them again. Candy felt a mix of grief and rage as she started to respond. That's when it happened. Jake picked up a hatchet that was lying on the ground and swung it with all his might at Adele's head. It sunk deep into her skull. For a moment she gave Candy a shocked, slightly startled look. Then her knees buckled and she slid backwards into the pool. The force of the blow sent the purse flying from her hand into some nearby Bougainvillea bushes. Candy looked in horror at her mother's body as it sank slowly beneath the crimson water, and then back at Jake. She grabbed the hatchet, threw it behind an adjacent Jacuzzi, took him by the wrist and headed out of the compound to her truck. She gunned the engine, drove to their motel, picked up their few belongings and was on the highway back to Vegas by 3 a.m.

21

Mike was at a loss. Nothing made sense. He had assumed the deaths were somehow connected, perhaps the work of a single killer. But now this. He sighed and picked up the Coroner's report again. It was very clear. The death of the big guy in the pool was from "natural causes". Nothing more complicated than a heart attack. The report did note a slight contusion on the skull but that was consistent with the claim by the old gay guy that he was trying to help and accidentally hit him on the head with the pole. It also noted the abrasions on his ass but they certainly were not the cause of death. In fact, it appeared this death had nothing to do with the previous murder. Which brought them back to square one.

It was so tantalizingly close. If the old gay man killed the guy there was reason to think he might be linked to the other deaths, although how remained a mystery. However, based on the coroner's report, there was no doubt the DA wouldn't proceed with charges and he would be released. So, who killed the old dyke by the pool at Caballeros Estates and who killed the bag lady three blocks away by the church? In each case the cause of death was a blow to the head. In the case of the dyke it was delivered by a hatchet that, as it turned out, belonged to the complex and was accidentally left out by the gardener. There were fingerprints on it but none that could be matched to anyone who might be a suspect. In the case of the homeless woman, it was a rock found a few feet from her body. And why was her body mutilated with the cactus?

The door opened and Zach walked in looking, as usual, like one of the Hardy boys on a treasure hunt.

"Hi boss, I think I may have something on the old queer, I mean the old gay guy who's our prime suspect. Apparently there was a killing in Provincetown a couple of years back when he was there. Some drag queen got his head bashed in by a rock."

Mike put his hand up to stop him. This was part of the problem. Zach was so keen that his certainty infected everyone else's judgement.

"We're going to have to let the old guy go."

Zach started to protest but Mike interrupted him.

"The Coroner ruled the cause of death a heart attack. There is no murder to solve."

"But what about the blow to the head?"

"Nothing serious and completely consistent with the guy's story. In fact, also consistent with what our witness saw even if he was someone we could rely on. There were the marks on the guy's ass but they didn't contribute to his death and I'm not sure we'll ever know what that was about, something we should probably be grateful for."

Zach winced and looked away.

"I expect the DA to drop charges this morning and the guy will be free to leave. But that still leaves us with two unsolved murders and absolutely no suspects."

Zach was deflated. All his certainties about this case depended on the little queer being the killer. It just made sense and, even better, supported his own views of right and wrong. He thought he was on the verge of breaking open a serial killer case and now he was left with what? Nothing. He put his hands in his pants pockets and left.

22

Candy followed developments in Palm Springs from the safety of her trailer in Los Vegas. She read about Adele's murder in the Desert Sun online as well as a second homicide at Caballeros Estates. The report said a suspect in the second death was in custody and police were working on the assumption that there may a connection between the two murders. Good news. She and Jake weren't on the radar.

What really got her attention, though, was Adele's obituary. It described her as a successful businesswoman and the owner of numerous properties throughout Palm Springs and the Coachella Valley. She was rich. The article indicated there was uncertainty as to the disposition of her estate and the authorities were looking for family members. Candy panicked. The prospect of her faggot brother inheriting the estate and leaving Candy and Jake with nothing made her furious. She regretted not grabbing the bag with the $10,000 but, by the sounds of the obituary, that was very small change indeed when compared to Adele's total worth.

They had to return to Palm Springs. Within hours she and Jake were back in the truck on the freeway heading south west. As she drove, Candy tried to form a plan. She knew Adele lived at Caballeros Estates. That was the place to start.

Once Candy and Jake had checked back into their Cathedral City motel they headed to Caballeros Estates. Adele's name was on the intercom along with her suite number. Jake jumped the fence and let his mother in. Although Adele's unit was locked, the dry wood of the frame caved to one kick by Jake. Inside, everything was in darkness.

Using a flashlight Candy carefully combed through her mother's home. In the second bedroom she found an unlocked filing cabinet. Inside, one file was marked "family". When she opened it she found no mention of herself, Jake or her father, just Mikey. Only he was no longer called Mikey. It also confirmed that he lived in Caballeros Estates in a unit owned by Adele. Candy's worst fears were realized. Her mother's heir was living in this very complex.

Jake called out from the living room where he had located the remnants of a computer, but no computer. As well, the shelves showed dust shadows where something had been removed.

There was a loud crash from the direction of the patio. Jake opened the door and examined the empty and dark patio. He heard something from beyond the wall and moved cautiously towards it. At first he saw nothing but darkness down below but then a tiny blinking light caught his attention and, before he could say or do anything, a shadowy figure leapt up and rushed out of sight. Candy and Jake hurried out the back door, down the stairs, across the courtyard and through the gate to their truck. The only thing Candy took was the file marked "family".

Lying in bed early the next morning Candy decided it might be worth searching the garbage/recycling bins at Caballeros Estates. She got Jake up and they headed back to the scene of last night's excitement. It was so early even the gardeners hadn't started work. The bins were both located outside the fenced perimeter and were accessed easily. Someone was there ahead of them. A binner was meticulously sorting through the recycling bin, laying its contents out on the surrounding asphalt.

"Morning" he said as they approached. He looked suspiciously at them, certain they were going to try to poach his treasures. "Fraid I've pulled out anything of value here. There's not much this morning, at least nothing like last week."

"What was there last week?" Candy asked.

"Well, I didn't get it, but the old gal who lives over by the church, I think her name is Maude, got quite a haul. There was an old computer and a box full of computer discs. She'll get quite a bit of money for them. I was hoping lightening might strike twice, but I guess not." He gave a tentative toothless grin.

"Where did you say this lady lives?"

"Well, not sure 'lives' is quite the right word, but she spends most of her time over by the Catholic church at Arenas and El Segundo. Not actually in the church although I think they let her use the bathroom. You can usually find her there in the afternoon when she's finished binning for the day."

Candy thanked him as they headed back to the truck.

Later that day Candy and Jake drove to the church. A funeral was in progress. People turned to look at the truck and they just kept driving. As they headed east, Candy caught site of a bag lady sitting on a fence watching the proceedings. Next to her was a large shopping cart filled with junk and covered by a tarp.

When they came back by the church two hours later everyone was gone, including the bag lady. They found signs of her habitation in the scrub brush beside the church but, otherwise, nothing.

The next morning Candy and Jake headed back to the church. That block of Arenas was completely deserted and silent under the scorching sun. As they passed the church they saw the bag lady walking into the scrub bush. Candy pulled over and she and Jake followed her.

"Maude?" Candy called out.

"Who wants to know?" said the bag lady as she turned her weathered and bloated face.

"A friend of yours sent us over here. We might like to buy some stuff from you."

A feral smile crossed Maude's face. She turned from Candy to Jake who was a couple of feet behind.

"And who is this sexy young man?" she purred in a girlish whisper. She ran her tongue around her lips and leered in his direction. It created the effect of a garish caricature from a Brueghel painting.

"He's Jake."

"Well, Jake honey, why don't you just come over here and get some nice pussy. " She swivelled her hips and made to lift her several stained and torn skirts.

Jake moved closer, a crazed look in his eyes and spittle dribbling from the corner of his mouth.

"Jake, honey, I think maybe you should go back to the truck."

Maude looked at Candy and then, again at Jake.

"What, a mamma's boy? I bet he's never even seen pussy, except yours." She let out a mucous inflected cackle.

"Look, all we want to do is talk with you about your stuff and maybe buy some of it."

It happened before Candy could finish her sentence. Jake picked up a large boulder and swung it at Maude's head. It landed with a sickening thud, sending a spray of blood in all directions. She collapsed. Before Candy could react, Jake grabbed Maude's skirts, pulled them over her head, picked up a broken piece of cactus and rammed it between her legs. He turned to his mother and gave her a twisted grin. His head was bobbing up and down. In the background Maude was writhing in the final spasms of life. She let out a gurgling sound and then went still.

Candy grabbed Jake by the sleeve and pulled him back to the truck. She pushed him in the passenger side, jumped in the driver's side and sped off.

Jeffery stared in disbelief at the paper in front of him. Even now, a week after its arrival, he couldn't fully absorb its content. He took a long sip from his martini and noted that Joan Sutherland was just then launching into the mad scene in Lucia di Lammermoor. How appropriate.

When the lawyer called, Jeffery thought it was one of his friends playing a tasteless joke but, as the conversation progressed, it became startlingly clear it was indeed a lawyer and he was dead serious. Jeffery went to the lawyer's office later that day where he was given a copy of the will and the covering letter that was now lying on his lap.

Adele was his mother. The words seemed simple enough but their implausibility defied easy comprehension. He barely remembered the woman who was his mother back in Vegas. Her name was Lucy and she disappeared mysteriously one night, never to be seen or heard from again. His father never talked about her to him but then his father mostly ignored him anyway except when, in drunken rages, he beat him up. All that was erased from his memory as he built a new life, with a new name. And now, out of the blue, it came surging back.

Not only was Adele his mother, her will named him her sole heir. She knew all along he was her son but never said anything to him. He remembered one time when he was sitting by the pool feeling someone staring at him and looking up to see Adele quickly turn away. What's more, she was his landlady. She owned this suite. Talk about a mix of emotions. Having obliterated all memory of his dysfunctional family, only to be confronted with the fact his own mother was near him for years and yet never identified herself, never once reached out to him, left him...what? Saddened? Angry? Certainly confused.

He wondered what the connection was between this news and the threatening note with the GI Joe doll.

When he returned from the lawyer's office Cora gave him a key to Adele's now vacant apartment. He felt he was an intruder as he let himself in to the life of this stranger. Nothing in the living room felt even remotely familiar. In the office he saw a laptop computer and a box of files. Awaiting him in the bedroom though was a shock. Next to the bed in an expensive metal frame was a yellowed photograph of a little boy. It was him. Jeffery choked up. He hurried out of the room and to the door. On his way out, he picked up the computer and the box of files.

And here he was, a week later, still trying to comprehend all that had happened. Sutherland was in full flight of madness now. He got up to make another martini.

****

The speed with which my life became my own again was dizzying. One moment I was a suspect in a murder, indeed in three, chained to Palm Springs by an ankle bracelet and branded with the mark of Cain by all the neighbours and the next, I was a free man. All charges involving Mat's death were dropped, the bracelet was removed and I was free to go home to Canada. The true north strong and free was never more inviting. The earliest I could get a flight to Vancouver without spending a fortune was three days after my release and I was due to leave at 8:00 tomorrow morning.

I really hadn't celebrated my exoneration. All I felt was relief. I missed John. Tonight seemed like the time to blow off a bit of steam, kick back and enjoy myself. Although I'm not much of a drinker, I do like my white wine so I went to Sidebar where they have quite decent happy hour chardonnay at a very reasonable price. I had a glass, actually two, and then went across to Rainbow where they have half price chicken wings and free meat balls during happy hour. I had another glass of wine there. By this time I was a bit tipsy so decided to head home. It still being light, I went down Arenas although my step certainly quickened as I passed the vacant lot where the dead bag lady was found. I noted for the umpteenth time the charming little sign in front of the church commemorating babies killed by abortions.

It was too early to turn in. I discovered an open bottle of wine in the fridge, one I had barely touched four days ago (one of the conditions of my bail was that I not drink alcohol so I had to be very careful at the time). I decided to go and sit in the Jacuzzi with my wine. In fact, I decided to be really daring and wear the lime green thong I purchased on impulse and never had the nerve to wear in public.

I glimpsed a reflection of myself in the mirror as I headed for the kitchen and was reminded that the thong left me quite exposed behind but, as long as I remembered to tighten my butt muscles, thought it quite attractive. Wrapping myself in a towel, I took a wine glass and the bottle and headed for the Jacuzzi by the central pool, assuming it would be quiet. There was no one around and darkness was falling so I shed the towel and got into the Jacuzzi with a minimum of fuss. As I poured myself a glass of wine, I was mindful that I was breaking the rule against glass in the pool areas but, having just been exonerated of a murder charge, this little infraction seemed inconsequential. The warm jets of water massaged the various nooks and crannies of my exhausted body as I settled back into the bubbling water. I drifted towards sleep.

****

As Jeffery poured his second (or was it third?) martini he heard the doorbell competing with La Stupenda's soprano. He opened the door and was confronted by two strangers who looked oddly familiar. In front was a woman a bit older than him with bleach blonde hair, leathery skin and feline eyes surrounded by heavy eyeliner. She was a blend of Goth and Annie Oakley. Behind her was a much more troubling visage: a youngish man whose head bobbed up and down and whose mouth was stretched in a kind of leer. His eyes were off kilter and his

skin was almost translucent where it stretched across bones protrud-
ing from his forehead. There was saliva dripping from one corner of
his mouth. Jeffery recognized him as the kid who was thrown out of
Sidebar. In the background Sutherland was shrieking:

Fuggita lo son de tuol numici!

un gelo me serpeggia nel sen!

trema ogni fibra!

"Yes? Can I help you?"

"I sure think you can Mikey."

"Mikey". Suddenly it hit him. His past. Vegas. His family or at least
his sister. But who was the crazed creature with her?

"My name is Jeffery. You must have the wrong address." He invol-
untarily stepped back as she advanced, a threatening leer on her face.

"No. Actually, I have the right address. You're Mikey, my long lost
faggot brother and I believe our dear departed mother has left you
a lot of money...or so I would guess. Now, I want my share or...". She
reached into her pocket and began to pull out a gun. Jeffery threw his
full martini, glass and all, in her face. He turned and ran through the
apartment, out onto the patio, through the gate and into the gardens.
La Stupenda had just completed her decent into madness.

****

All the stress of the last few weeks drained away as the warm water
washed over my body and the wine insinuated itself through my blood.
I drifted in and out of consciousness. High above, the crows were caw-
ing and, somewhere nearby, desert doves cooed. Paradise was found.

Suddenly there was a commotion to my left. I heard shouts against
a backdrop of opera, undoubtedly coming from the opera queen's
home over there, then the sounds of footsteps running in my direction
and finally several short pops, rather like a car backfiring. Before I
could react a frantic Jeffery ran right by me heading in the direction of
the parking garage. He was so focussed on running he didn't even cast
a glance in my direction. A very troubling looking woman appeared
in hot pursuit right behind him. She was brandishing a gun and just

as she passed the Jacuzzi fired it in the air. Good god, the pops were shots. I froze, hoping she would not notice me as she hurried by. The immediate threat seemed to have passed when more footsteps began beating in my direction. An even stranger looking person rushed out of the darkness and hurried by, again without looking down at the Jacuzzi where I was suddenly anything but relaxed.

Another shot was fired, followed by shouting. Then the sky fell. No, I mean it. Literally, the sky fell. There I was sitting in the Jacuzzi, practically naked, and a great black thing fell into the tub with me. Naturally I screamed. The strange person, who had nearly disappeared into the garage by then, stopped and looked back. He was one of the oddest looking men I have ever laid eyes upon…and that's saying something. I didn't know what was more worrying, his noticing me or this large creature now flopping around in the hot tub with me as the water turned a very disturbing shade of pink. He drew a knife and headed back towards me, pausing a few steps from the Jacuzzi with an evil smile on his face.

The relaxing Jacuzzi had changed into a pot of boiling water and I was being prepared for dinner by a cannibal. Apparently it was going to be a major feast, including the large dark bird that had fallen in with me. As if to complete this hideous tableau, I spilled my wine into the water. It was going to be a gourmet feast.

I may be sixty six but I was quite athletic in my younger years, in fact, quite an accomplished ballet dancer, and with one leap (in ballet we call it a grand jete'), I cleared the Jacuzzi and hit the ground running towards the main gate. He was in hot pursuit and, although it didn't sound very butch, I screamed for help at the top of my lungs all the while running practically naked towards the front gate of the complex.

Cora was out on her patio enjoying her last cigarette of the day and reflecting on the beautiful calm desert evening when she heard the shots. They were followed by screams that sounded familiar. She called 911 and headed in the direction of the noise.

I got to the gate and fumbled with the lock. He was fast approaching behind me and I had visions of being eviscerated up against the gate, my mangled body clothed only in the lime green thong. After what seemed like an eternity, it finally opened and I dashed out into the driveway, the gate slamming behind me. I didn't know which way to turn but that concern resolved itself quickly as first one and then many police cars came screaming up the driveway.

As Mike pulled the squad car into the driveway of Caballeros Estates he was greeted by the extraordinary sight of the old gay guy running towards his headlights, naked except for a tiny green swimsuit of sorts. His arms were flapping in all directions. His eyes were dilated and he was screaming at the top of his lungs. Mike stopped, drew his gun and leapt out of the car just as the other police cars arrived.

The cops jumped out with their guns drawn and someone shone a spot light on me. Suddenly I was very naked. Behind me the gate opened and closed as my pursuer advanced. The spotlight shifted to him, there was some running about, a cry or two and he was on the ground in handcuffs. The next thing I knew Cora was at my side and I was trying to explain what was going on inside the complex but the more I talked the more hysterical I became. She let the police in and they fanned out looking for the shooter. The nasty young cop who interrogated me remained with us. I didn't dare think what was going through his head as I backed up against a car so as not to expose my naked bottom. Despite the sun having been down for some hours, the car was startlingly hot.

There were shouts from the back of the complex, two further shots and then silence. After a few minutes the older police officer appeared, leading the scary woman who was now handcuffed. Behind her with the other officers was Jeffery, white as a sheet and having difficulty walking.

Epilogue

The first rays of morning sun filtered through the palm grove and illuminated the tranquil scene below. The clear blue water of the pools shimmered. Humming birds hovered around hibiscus blossoms and two doves strutted back and forth on a fence, cooing their affection for each other. An angry caw came from high up in the palm trees as the lone crow stared down at her mate floating lifeless in the Jacuzzi.

The End of Book One

About the Author

G eoff Holter is a frustrated writer. He attended both the University of British Columbia and Simon Fraser University and has two degrees in English. He has just retired from a long career where he helped rich people get even richer. He lives in Vancouver, Canada with his two best friends, Tad and Scudder.

CPSIA information can be obtained at www.ICGtesting.com
Printed in the USA
LVOW05s2044220114

370541LV00025B/920/P

9 781492 278863